What the critics are saying about...

Naughty Girl

"Ms. McKenna has created a tale filled with suspense and romance that will thrill readers of erotica...a fast paced read that is beyond enjoyable!" – *Angie, Love Romances*

"J.W. McKenna has written a beautiful story of submission between two people in the story of Carl and DeeDee...Their scenes together just talking were very well written and the sex was HOT!" – *Julie Esparza, Just Erotic Romance Reviews*

Darkest Hour

"J.W. McKenna has written more than just a story of sexual submission. She has written one woman's story of need and determination. A man and a woman who will not be denied." – *Shadoe Simmons, The Best Reviews.com*

The Hunted

"The Hunted features two deliciously interesting stories of women being hunted and captured. I thoroughly enjoyed both stories and was fascinated with each of the author's characters." – *Michelle Gann, The Word on Romance*

Lord of Avalon

"McKenna's story is full of compassionate characters, unashamed of their desires and sincerely concerned with others' well-being. Overall, Lord of Avalon is a wonderful book, fairly short in length, but with a rich story." – *Marliese Thomas, Romance Reviews Today*

Slave Planet

"This is a fantastic, sexy tale, filled with strong women who know that they want and are not afraid to take it." – *Amy Turpin, Timeless Tales*

Wanted: Kept Woman

"What I thought would be a cute read turned into much more. J.W. McKenna has written a story that grabs your attention and doesn't let go until the last word. It has something for everyone: laughter, found love, suspense and a little sex thrown in." – *Claudia McRay, Romance Junkies*

NAUGHTY GIRL

J. W. McKenna

NAUGHTY GIRL
An Ellora's Cave Publication, November 2004

Ellora's Cave Publishing, Inc.
PO Box 787
Hudson, OH 44236-0787

ISBN #1419950894

Other available formats: Microsoft Reader (LIT), Adobe (PDF), Rocketbook (RB), Mobipocket (PRC) & HTML

Edited by Sue Ellen Gower
Cover art by Syneca

Warning:

The following material contains graphic sexual content meant for mature readers. *Naughty Girl* has been rated E–rotic by a minimum of three independent reviewers.

Ellora's Cave Publishing offers three levels of Romantica™ reading entertainment: S (S-ensuous), E (E-rotic), and X (X-treme).

S-*ensuous* love scenes are explicit and leave nothing to the imagination.

E-*rotic* love scenes are explicit, leave nothing to the imagination, and are high in volume per the overall word count. In addition, some E-rated titles might contain fantasy material that some readers find objectionable, such as bondage, submission, same sex encounters, forced seductions, etc. E-rated titles are the most graphic titles we carry; it is common, for instance, for an author to use words such as "fucking", "cock", "pussy", etc., within their work of literature.

X-*treme* titles differ from E-rated titles only in plot premise and storyline execution. Unlike E-rated titles, stories designated with the letter X tend to contain controversial subject matter not for the faint of heart.

NAUGHTY GIRL

J. W. McKenna

Chapter One

She'd come into the downtown Santa Barbara bar that night with a man who oozed money. Carl Harman immediately pegged her as a gold digger—how could he not, the way they were so mismatched? He could see the same thought in the eyes of the other single men in the crowded bar.

Honey-Blonde—which was how Carl thought of her at first—was young and sexy while her companion was older and more oily. His body, once muscular, had gone soft. His thinning black hair was combed straight back over beady eyes. His only saving grace was a row of white, even teeth, perfect for a false smile. He reminded Carl of a used car salesman. To attract a gal like that, he had to be loaded. Women who'd trade their youth for old money usually didn't interest Carl. But she was the exception.

Car Salesman led her to the bar a couple of stools down from Carl and ordered a stiff scotch for himself and a white wine for her. The man spoke in a loud voice and seemed to treat the girl like an accessory.

Carl, sitting at the bar nursing his drink, tried not to pay attention to her. That quickly proved to be impossible when he noticed she wasn't wearing a bra under her gray silk blouse. He could see the round shape of her breasts and the hint of her nipples. She was in her late twenties and had medium-sized breasts, so she didn't really need a bra. Still, a woman who walked into a bar braless made

Carl wonder about what else she might be missing underneath her navy blue wrap-around skirt.

Now that she had his full attention, he took in other details. She stood about five-seven, so Carl, at six feet, imagined that he wouldn't have to lean over too far to kiss her, and her perfectly heart-shaped ass would be at just the right height to run his fingers over it. His hand itched at the mere thought. Her face reminded him vaguely of Faye Dunaway in her prime—beautiful blue eyes, strong cheekbones and jaw, although softer somehow, more demure. Her honey-blonde hair seemed natural to Carl, though he wondered if the drapes matched the carpet. He smiled at his own crude joke and took another sip of his martini.

Carl noticed that when Car Salesman wasn't looking, the young woman's eyes glanced about the room as if she were searching for someone. Only later did he find out she was looking for someone to rescue her—or why she couldn't rescue herself.

Car Salesman proceeded to get drunk in short order. Perhaps he could tell that his grip on Honey-Blonde was slipping and he was determined to be a real horse's ass before it all ended. Or perhaps he just couldn't help himself—maybe he treated everybody this way. Carl minded his own business, nursing his drink.

He was in-between girlfriends at the moment and feeling a little sorry for himself. He'd been idly thinking about renting a video on the way home. After he spotted Honey-Blonde, he thought perhaps an adult video might be better. She had that effect on him. He never expected he'd get any closer to her than he was at that moment, two stools down in a bar full of TGIF'ers.

But when Car Salesman suddenly tossed the remains of his drink on her and, in a loud voice, accused her of flirting, the White Knight in Carl woke up. Everyone else seemed to stare then edged away, as if they didn't want to get involved in a lovers' quarrel. Or maybe Car Salesman's sudden rage made them fearful. Though going to seed, he still had the look of a brawler.

Carl couldn't stand it. He came off his stool and approached them before he was even aware he had moved.

"Hey, now," he said, trying to be chivalrous without seeming like he was trying to steal Honey-Blonde away because, frankly, he wasn't at that moment.

Then he saw her sad, tired expression and how the man's drink had splashed over her chest, causing her left nipple to show clearly through the sheer material. Carl fell just a little bit in love with her right then.

Car Salesman turned his sudden fury on Carl. "Mind your own fuckin' bizness or I'll shove your head up your ass."

He made Carl instantly angry. He struggled to get a firm grip on his temper. It was as if an avalanche was being held back by a single log against a rock. He strained to hold that log in place.

Carl turned his eyes fully on the man and gave him his best "Don't-Fuck-With-Me" look. But the man was too drunk to notice. In fact, Carl believed he was itching for a fight. Perhaps, long ago, he had rescued Honey-Blonde from another old, drunk Alpha Male and thought he might regain some of his power by defeating some upstart.

"Where I come from," Carl said evenly, "men don't throw drinks at the ladies. It's usually the other way around." He could feel the log shift against the rock in his head.

Now if Car Salesman had laughed, or calmed down or apologized to the woman, the moment would have passed, and that would've been the end of it. But somehow Carl knew none of those things would happen. Something evil flickered in the man's eyes and the tumblers in his drunken brain seemed to click into place.

The man reared back, so Carl saw the punch coming from about a half-mile away. Maybe ten years ago and maybe if the man wasn't drunk, he might've been able to catch him with it. Carl doubted it, but he was trying to be kind. He had about a half-hour to decide which way to lean to avoid the callused hand and how to place his feet to get the maximum power into his own punch. As Car Salesman's fist creaked by him—no doubt lightning speed from his vantage point—Carl popped him a good one right in the nose and stepped back.

Car Salesman wasn't sure he'd been hurt until he felt the blood spill out onto his shirt. He clamped a hand to his face and howled, his eyes already beginning to water. Focusing all his hatred in Carl's direction, Salesman wanted to kill him, to dismember him, but Carl could tell he suddenly realized he was at a disadvantage—Carl wasn't the pushover he'd thought he was. Carl could see his mind working. Mentally, he begged him to back down as he strained to hold his avalanche of anger in check.

But no. Car Salesman's eyes cast about for a weapon— a harpoon, a howitzer—anything massive enough to end this fight quickly and with maximum damage. Carl believed the man was fully prepared to kill him in that moment.

The drunk lunged to his right and grabbed a chair from an empty table. It was one of those wood and wicker jobs that weigh about twelve pounds—hardly the right choice, although it would've stung quite a bit to be hit with it. Apparently it was all he could manage on the spur of the moment.

Carl almost shook his head as he mentally kicked the log free and allowed the rush of anger and adrenaline to overtake him. The light took on a reddish tint. His vision narrowed to include only the angry drunk in front of him. Car Salesman's already slow reaction time became glacial in Carl's accelerated vision. Before he had that chair up high enough to smash him in the head, Carl had chopped him up with three quick strikes. Left to the head, right to the stomach, then pivoted into a right uppercut. He followed with a leg sweep and a shoulder push that sent the drunk crashing to the floor.

He didn't get up. Carl really wanted him to. He thought seriously about kicking him a few times, but he resisted the urge. Slowly, the red haze cleared and he became more aware of the rest of the room.

He turned to the man's wide-eyed companion. *God, she was beautiful,* he thought all over again. "Are you all right?"

Carl wondered if she was one of those women who immediately would fall to their companion's side, regardless of how he'd treated her, and rail against the bully who hurt him.

She seemed stunned. She looked down at her groaning companion, then up at Carl, then down at her nipple that was doing its best to poke through the material of her blouse. She didn't answer at first, as if trying to sort out her emotions. She reached down and plucked the blouse away from her breast. Carl was sorry to see her nipple go.

She bit her lip, looking like a lost little girl. "Umm, I guess. I...I..."

She didn't seem to know what to say about it. She was rescued by the bartender, who finally managed to lumber out from behind the bar and came to where they were standing over the prone figure.

"What'dja do, kill 'im?" He was a beefy guy, with long black hair tied in a ponytail. In his right hand, he carried a Little League-sized Louisville Slugger. The barman's special.

"No," Carl responded. "I think he's more drunk than hurt." At least he hoped that was true. He looked up at Honey-Blonde. "I didn't want to hurt him." *The hell I didn't*, he thought. Her eyes were wide and Carl could see tears brimming in them.

"I saw it—he came at you with a fuckin' chair. He had it coming." The bartender turned to the woman. "Whaddya wanna do? You wanna call the cops? An ambulance? Or shall we just get him back to his car?" It was clear which choice *he* preferred.

Honey-Blonde glanced from Car Salesman to Carl then back again. He could feel those pale blue eyes on him. She seemed to make a decision.

When she finally spoke, her voice was soft. "It's all right," she told the bartender. "My friend and I can take him from here." Carl thought his heart would burst—"my friend" she had called him!

He nodded dumbly. The bartender shrugged and moved away, the small baseball bat tapping against his meaty thigh. The noise in the bar began to return to normal. All those Yuppies grateful that the crisis had passed. No one was asking them to defend *their* women, thank god. Now they could get back to cursing the economy, and lying about their past successes over blended drinks.

With the sagging, semiconscious body of Car Salesman between them, Honey-Blonde and Carl horsed him out the door to a black Mercedes parked in a handicapped space. Carl thought it ironic that the man had parked illegally in the handicapped spot going into the bar, but fully qualified for it on the way out. The drunk didn't fight them. He seemed happy to have the help.

The woman fished in Car Salesman's front pocket for his keys and thumbed the button to unlock the doors. Carl expected her to pile him into the back seat, thank him for his help then drive off out of his life. He was amazed when she directed him to dump the drunk across the front seats, tossing the keys in after him.

She shut the door and turned her hundred-watt heat on Carl. "Will you take me home?"

"Um, yeah, sure, you bet." He tried not to sound like Elmer Fudd. He had many questions: *Do you live with him? What do you see in him? Are you in love with him?* But he said nothing else.

Carl directed her to his aging Honda, embarrassed as he mentally compared it to the luxury vehicle she had arrived in. He opened the door for her and silently thanked the heavens he had cleaned out the old fast food wrappers just three days prior.

"Where to?" he asked as he eased himself into the driver's seat.

"Montecito."

Carl nodded. He should've guessed. Montecito was the exclusive part of Santa Barbara. Old money, new money and lots of security guards. He figured she was directing him to Car Salesman's house, where no doubt she lived like a pretty bird in a gilded cage.

Carl drove, casting about for something, anything to say. She seemed to be in shock. He wondered if the sudden violence turned her off, or if she considered him dangerous.

"Look, I'm sorry about all that. I shouldn't've hit him so hard." He meant it. One punch probably would've been enough, considering how drunk the man had been. He was going to have a headache, that's for sure.

"He had it coming," she said bitterly. There was a lot of weight behind that one sentence.

"Has he thrown a drink on you before?"

"Sure. Or worse. It's been coming apart for a while now."

Carl decided not to ask for the gory details. Time for a change of subject. "You live in Montecito long?"

"Two years. I'm not actually in Montecito. More like on the edge."

"With that guy?" *Shit!* Carl couldn't help himself.

"What? Him? No way," The emotion behind her words lifted his hopes. "He's just someone I've been seeing."

"Well, it's a shame he treated you that way. I doubt you deserved it."

"No, I didn't. No one does," she said sharply.

"Yeah, that's what I meant," he jumped in, trying to cover up his gaffe. He hoped he didn't come across as a sexist pig.

He tried to change the subject. "My name's Carl. Carl Harman."

"Diedra Newman. My friends—" She stopped.

"Your friends?" he prompted.

"Never mind. Here, turn left at the next light." She directed him to an apartment complex lining the main street near Montecito. Carl could see the big brass gates of an exclusive complex from the where he parked. Close enough to get some benefit from the additional security up the road. That told him these apartments probably weren't cheap.

That made him think of Car Salesman again and whether he was paying her rent. "Let me walk you up, okay? I'm worried that your friend might wake up and be mad at you." It was half the truth and half a ploy to see her apartment. She might even invite him in.

He held his breath while she thought about it. He figured she knew the score. She was an attractive—hell, gorgeous—woman whom he had just rescued. Diedra probably thought he was just another horny man, expecting a quick fuck in return. Carl wasn't so crass, but she did turn him on. How could she not?

Diedra turned her wattage on him again, only this time, he could feel the yellow warning lights. "Look. You've been very nice to help me. I hope you understand that I'm kinda all mixed up right now. I don't want to, um, start something."

Carl held up his hands. "I understand completely, Diedra. I'm not expecting anything. I'm genuinely concerned about you. Yes, I admit that I'd like to get to know you better, but that's as far as my thinking goes right now."

You liar, he thought. *Given the chance, you'd jump her bones in a minute.*

Again, he pictured her little brown nipple, pressing against her gray blouse. Carl willed his eyes not to look at it and succeeded, right up until she glanced out the windshield. Then he peeked and was disappointed to see the drink had dried, leaving just a little brownish stain on her blouse. Her nipple had made its retreat. He hoped he had managed to raise his eyes before she turned back.

"Okay, but just until I'm safely inside. I am kinda shook up." She opened the door before he could get around to her side of the car. Carl stayed close, but not too close, as they strolled up the walkway to the arched entryway. He could smell her perfume, a soft, enticing fragrance that wasn't helping his Boy Scout demeanor. His cock stirred.

"I'm here, to the left." She pointed.

He tried not to pant like a horndog as he followed along. They came to a red door, number 136 in gold numerals on it. Carl was sure he could find it again during a power outage in the middle of a rainstorm with wild dogs chasing him.

"Well, this is it." She turned toward him. Her body posture seemed dismissive, and yet... He sensed she liked him.

"Diedra, despite the rather ugly circumstances, it's been a real pleasure to meet you. I hope you'll forgive me for hurting your boyfriend, although he doesn't deserve someone like you."

She smiled and he almost took a step back. Her powerful charisma washed over him. As it was, Carl rocked on his heels a little. His cock began to press against his jeans.

Down, Simba! Not now!

"Well, thank you. You've really been nice. A real gentleman. And for the record, he's not my boyfriend. Not anymore."

"That's very good to hear, but he might have different ideas." Carl hesitated, then took the plunge. "But if you two don't get back together, would you object if I called you up and took you out sometime?"

She actually blushed. His dream-girl blushed! She looked down at the ground.

"I don't know," she said in that bedroom voice. Carl waited, his heart beating rapidly. "I'm still all mixed up." She glanced up at his earnest face and seemed to soften. "Well, maybe."

Carl's head seemed to leave his shoulders. "S-sure." He shifted position to conceal his growing erection. If Diedra noticed, she paid no attention. Carl felt he was carrying a surfboard in his pants.

"Let me give you my phone number." She parted her full lips, waiting for him to get ready.

He reached into his pants pocket—careful, careful!— for a pen and he saw her gaze briefly drop, then snap up again as if she didn't want him to catch her looking. Carl felt a flush of embarrassment creep up from his neck to his cheeks. He tried to adjust his pants to hide his erection and looked up to see redness creep up her neck as well. He made a big deal out of writing the number down on his palm, trying to cover up the awkward moment.

Diedra gave him the number, one digit at a time, at such a low pitch, Carl had to lean in to hear her. Her perfume mixed with the real woman odor of her and it triggered an animalistic reaction. All he wanted to do at that exact moment was thrust her up against the door, raise her skirt and see if his suspicions about her lack of panties were true. If they were, he wanted to take her right then and there. Carl tried not to shake as he wrote down the final digits.

Forcing himself to step back to keep his sanity, he started to write down her name over the number, for no reason other than to stall for time. When she reached out to touch his arm, he knew she felt some of that animal lust as well. It was as if she didn't want him to move too far away. She wanted to prolong the moment just a little longer. Or so he hoped.

"How do you spell Diedra?" he asked, though he easily could've guessed.

Her lips parted. She licked them, a soft pink tongue caressing softer red lips. For some strange reason, he imagined them around the head of his cock and had to close his eyes against the image.

"Actually, my friends call me DeeDee."

"DeeDee…that's a nice name." She could've said Bertha or Agnes and he'd have said the same thing. "A very nice name."

He'd run out of things to stall about. He let his hand drop to his side. He wouldn't wash it until that number was copied down in his little black book. His very thin little black book. His very thin little black book with moths flying out of it.

It had been a slow year.

"Well, I guess that's it. You should be safe now, I expect. He probably won't wake up until morning anyway." Carl's mind cast about for some other reason to stand there, talking. He grasped a sliver of an idea. "Of course, if he comes by and he's really angry, you could call me. I mean, if you wanted to."

Or she could call the police, you complete idiot!

DeeDee smiled again and it took all his concentration not to puddle at her feet like a schoolboy. "Sure. That would be real nice. But I don't think it will come to that."

"Just in case." Carl started to give her his number then realized she had nothing to write on. He wouldn't expect her to write it on her palm—that was far too crude for such an elegant woman.

She hesitated then began looking through her tiny purse for some scrap of paper and found none. Carl could see the wheels turning in her head. Did she invite him in or did she just tell him to forget the number for now, she'd get it later? Carl held his breath. His hard-on held its breath. The world stopped spinning on its axis.

Perhaps his earnest good looks helped her decide. "Okay, come in for a minute and let me get some paper. Just for a minute, you understand."

Yes, Virginia, there is a Santa Claus.

Carl kept his face neutral, as if this meant nothing. His erection knew better. It swelled another notch. If she'd misplaced her keys, he could've used it as a battering ram against the door.

She unlocked the door and led the way inside. Carl shuffled in behind her, giving his crotch a glaring look when her back was turned. *Not now!* She turned on a lamp by the couch.

Her apartment had a casual look to it. A few newspapers and magazines lay scattered over the coffee table and the sofa, but it was otherwise well kept. The rug had recently been vacuumed, he could tell from the machine marks on the nap. Looking through the doorway into her darkened kitchen, Carl could see the table was clear of dirty dishes, yet there were a couple of cups and a plate on the counter near the coffee maker.

"Excuse the mess," she said and he wanted to tell her, *no, darling, it's perfect, just like you,* but he said nothing.

She found a piece of paper and handed it to him. He carefully wrote down "Carl Harman" and the number in block figures so it would be easy to read. "There you go." He handed it over. Fortunately, the cerebral act of writing helped diminish his cock somewhat. At least it was no longer threatening to take over the city like Godzilla.

They stood there for several seconds. Carl wanted to stay and he suspected she wanted him to, yet there was nothing else he could do to delay the inevitable.

"Well," he said, and let it hang. Carl reached out and took her hand gently into his. It was almost hot to the touch. "I've really enjoyed meeting you." He gave her hand a little squeeze.

He let it go and turned toward the door, defeated.

"Wait."

He turned back, expectantly.

"You, um, you had a drink on the bar, I remember."

He nodded. "A martini." Carl struggled to think of something else. "I usually drink beer at home, but when I go out, I like martinis."

Oh, great! Give her a rundown on my exciting alcohol choices! What next? I like a dry white wine with my fish?

"But you didn't get to finish it. You left it when Frank tossed his drink at me."

So that was the car salesman's name. Frank. Frank the Fuck-up.

Carl waved a hand, ready to dismiss it as nothing then caught himself. *She's giving you an opening, you big fat idiot!* Then something else occurred to him. *She noticed a little detail like that? The drink I had on the bar? She must've been paying attention to me long before Frank went into his act!*

"Um, would you like to go out for a drink?" He checked his watch. It was just past eleven-thirty. "The night's still young."

She looked coy and a little uncertain, as if she couldn't believe she was doing this. "I have the makings for martinis right here, if that's all right."

All right? *All right!?* Like telling a kid it was all right if he wanted to run into a toy store and buy something. Or, more aptly, telling a tiger it was all right if he wanted to devour a gazelle. His semi-erect cock roared back to full alert status. Def-con 2. Carl thought it would poke out over his belt buckle. If it got any bigger, she'd run screaming from the room.

"That would be lovely." *Lovely? Do real men say lovely?*

She turned, and for a moment in the lamplight, the way her skirt covered her shapely ass, he could've sworn she wasn't wearing panties. He wondered if he would ever find out for sure, this night or any other.

"Make yourself at home," she said over her shoulder. She went into the kitchen and fussed about. Carl heard glasses clinking and ice clanking. He didn't know if he should stay in the living room or follow her into the kitchen. He decided to stay put and pressed his hand hard against his cock, trying to get it to calm down, just a little.

Later, I might need you, buddy! Not now! You're embarrassing me!

He could tell DeeDee was nervous. *Hell,* Carl told himself, *I'm nervous — and I'm old enough to have done this a few times before.*

Somehow, DeeDee was different. He couldn't explain why.

Carl stood near the couch and let his eyes roam about the room. She had a bookcase and he moved closer so he could read some of the authors' names. Kipling, Frost, Updike, Keats — a wide and literate selection of writers and poets. Down lower, there were the usual women's self-help books: "How to Find a Good Man", "What Men Want" and "Understanding the Male Animal". Carl smiled. He believed books about men used one hundred thousand words to explain what can be said in just six: Food, Work, Booze, Sports, Sex and Cars. Not necessarily in that order.

She came back with a false gaiety, her movements a bit too jerky, and for a moment, Carl was afraid his presence was starting to spook her. He could see it from her point of view — a stranger rescues her, but is he really a White Knight or just a Black Knave in disguise? She'd probably met too many Black Knaves in her life.

He took the proffered drink, then reached out and touched her forearm. She flinched.

"It's all right. I'm nervous too." He stopped, trying to organize his words as if he were negotiating world peace. "I find you compelling, DeeDee. I wouldn't do anything to upset you." Carl put his drink down on the coffee table, making sure he used a coaster to show he was civilized. "If it would make you feel more comfortable, I can leave right now and we can try again later. Maybe go on a formal date."

That stopped her. The words seemed to comfort her. "No. No, it's all right. I...I admit I'm a little nervous. This is happening so suddenly. I don't know you very well and suddenly, you're in my apartment."

"I'm not like Frank." *What a lame thing to say*, he thought. *I am such a jerk.*

"I know. I could tell. It's just all so sudden."

"Sure." Carl picked up his drink and took a sip. "Let's just get to know each other, okay?" In his pants, he could swear he heard his cock scoff. It withered in disgust.

She gave him a tentative smile. It was enough. "Okay. You start."

Carl would rather talk about her, so he gave her the short version of his life. "I was born in Fresno to a schoolteacher and a county employee," he said, falling into his one-minute biography. "After an unexciting childhood, I went to Berkeley on a scholarship."

She leaned forward slightly and he immediately shut up. Any man would.

"What kind of scholarship?"

"Football. I was a wide receiver."

Carl could tell she was checking out his arms. He resisted the urge to flex his biceps. A little smile graced the edge of her soft pink mouth.

"I thought all wide receivers were black."

"Yeah, it seems like that now, doesn't it? But there were a few of us. Especially at Berkeley."

"Didn't go to the pros?"

"Nope. Wasn't good enough."

"Sorry—I didn't mean to pry."

"It's all right. It's just the way it was."

"So what do you do now?"

Carl sighed. He wanted to tell her everything, and yet, what would she think?

"I'm, um, a writer." Okay, that was only partially true, he told himself.

"Ohh, you mean like a novelist?"

"Sort of," he admitted, as if it were painful.

"Why so shy about it?"

"Because I haven't sold anything of substance yet. Some articles. I'm working on a book. Mostly, during the day, I work, um, on other things."

DeeDee sat back. "Doing what?" She wasn't going to let him off the hook.

"Graphic artist and, um, copywriter."

He expected her to suddenly realize he was small potatoes. Carl felt out of her league. A graphic artist couldn't afford a stunning woman like this. Then again, she must already know this—she'd seen his cheap car.

Instead, she seemed intrigued. "What kind of work do you do?"

Encouraged, Carl told her about some recent projects. A web site for a Realtor, a print ad for a landscaper, and a mascot mouse for the city library.

"Oh, I saw that one!" she exclaimed.

"You did?" Of course, he thought, she has all those books. She probably goes to the library a lot.

"Yes, I really liked it. You did that?"

"Yep." He was amazed that Literate Mouse had registered with this beautiful woman. "I'm working on a companion now, a girl mouse named Romantic Mouse. She's designed to show female readers that there's a lot of romance in the classics, if they'd just take the time to read them."

"Oh, don't I know! I love the classics."

Carl noted that his cock had completely faded, no doubt bored with this literary talk, but his brain was now fully engaged. They began to talk about many of the great books they'd read and enjoyed. Carl remained aware of her beauty, but now knew she was also his intellectual equal. It was a rare package indeed.

He suspected DeeDee felt it too. Her concerns about him seemed to melt away. The conversation began to flow more easily. After his first martini, he refused more, worried that he might appear too much like drunken Frank. Carl was never a big drinker anyway, so he didn't want to give her that impression.

"What about you?" he asked. "What do you do?"

She looked away for a moment, then said vaguely, "Oh, I have some investments."

He didn't want to let it go like that. Did that mean she was rich or perhaps "kept" by her rich boyfriends? "Investments? You mean, stocks and bonds..." he hesitated, "...or something else?"

Her eyes met his. "You mean, am I a dot.com millionaire? No. Mostly it's just boring old stocks and bonds. Not many, really—just enough to keep the rent paid."

Carl was curious to find out how she got to that point. Did she have a method? Did she inherit them from her parents? Or did a sugar daddy give them to her?

"You must be a good stock-picker," he offered, to see if she'd rise to the bait.

But DeeDee only shrugged. "Not really. Most of them I inherited."

"Oh, so your parents, um, have passed on?" Carl couldn't believe how hard it was to get her to talk about herself.

"My mom's still alive," she said, taking a small sip of her drink. Carl felt he'd pressed her far enough on an obviously sensitive topic, so he dropped it.

The woman has some money and it's none of my fucking business.

He sensed a lull in the conversation and felt it was time to go. He would have jumped at the chance to make love to her, but he knew it was the wrong move. She had a lot of heat and a lot of heart, and Carl wanted both fully engaged. If his flaccid cock had arms, it would've raised them in disgust.

"I should go," he told her, standing up. "I've really enjoyed meeting you. I would love to take you out for dinner."

"Really? That'd be nice." She stood as well.

"How about tomorrow?" Carl looked at his watch, then grinned. It was well past midnight. "No, tonight?"

"Um." She frowned. "Yes, I think I can arrange that. Frank was supposed to take me out, but he's lost the privilege. I would like to go with you."

"Listen, if he gives you any trouble, let me know, okay?"

"What—you'll beat him up again?"

Inwardly, Carl cringed. He didn't want to come across as a macho man. "No, no, nothing like that. I meant, if you have to talk to him, go out with him, we can do it another day."

She smiled that radiant smile again. "No. I'd rather go with you. Unless you plan on getting drunk and abusive on me."

Carl shook his head. "Won't happen. Ever." He leaned in suddenly to kiss her on the cheek.

She surprised him by turning her head so their lips met. They were everything he expected from her—hot, supple and full of promise. He could kiss those lips all day. Carl took advantage of their clutch to answer a question he'd had all night. He let his right hand lay upon her hip and could tell immediately she wasn't wearing any panties.

Simba reawakened and roared his approval.

Chapter Two

"God, what am I getting myself into?" DeeDee asked her reflection as she touched up her makeup in the bathroom mirror. The woman staring back at her seemed nervous. Her eyes were wide. She licked her lips then had to redo her lipstick.

She couldn't explain her sudden attraction to Carl. It was more than just physical appearance. Sure, he was nice to look at — tall, with those wide shoulders tapering into narrow hips. A handsome face with kind eyes. Maybe it was the way he carried himself. He exuded a certain confidence. And power. Like in the way he'd handled Frank. She had been shocked, but it had been over before she could react. Carl had stopped as soon as Frank had fallen down, as if he had control of the situation. DeeDee remembered how wet she had suddenly become. She had been sure he could smell her arousal.

Isn't that so trite, reacting to a strong man that way?

Control. A dangerous drug in the wrong hands. Frank wielded control like a weapon. She had been attracted to it at first. It satisfied her longing. Yet Frank quickly went to the dark side, especially when he drank, which was often. Instead of using it as a sexual stimulant, Frank turned it against her. If Carl hadn't come along, she would've tried to end it anyway. Whether she could have pried herself free of Frank's clutches or not had been the question.

So Carl had stepped in and saved her, and now she might find herself right back where she started. Unless Carl was different. After all, few men were like Stephen.

Tears came to her eyes at the thought of her old lover and she cursed under her breath. She daubed her eyeliner, trying to keep from smearing the makeup. "I don't have time for this!" she told her reflection. She checked her watch. 6:45. He'd be here in just a few minutes.

Think of something else!

That didn't help. She couldn't help but think of Stephen now. Felt doomed to keep searching for a man who could both thrill and protect her like he had. Someone in whose arms she felt safe, even when he was demanding so much of her.

She shook her head. DeeDee didn't need a psychiatrist to tell her where this came from. Her father. He'd been a wonderful father to her and a loving husband to her mother. A very strong man, but in a good way. He had believed in discipline. If she got bad grades or if she was willful, she got spanked. The spankings hurt, but she found herself enjoying them, too, in a strange, perverse way. She couldn't explain the emotions that had welled up inside her. Sometimes, she would do something wrong just to feel his broad, flat hand on her bottom. He never used a brush or a belt, yet DeeDee thought about the possibilities more than once.

Overall, her father had supported and encouraged her, allowing her to grow up into a well-adjusted, pretty, twelve-year-old girl, gaining confidence even as her body changed.

Twelve years. That was all the time they'd been given. It wasn't nearly enough. The memories flooded back, like snapshots. Dad, swinging her in the backyard swing set he'd put up himself. Dad, eyes misty as DeeDee had blown out the candles on her birthday cake. Dad, walking along the trail beside her during a Girl Scout hike at the park.

Mom had been there too, of course. But in the presence of Dad, she seemed smaller somehow. Not in a bad way. She had loved her husband as much as DeeDee did. She just preferred to let him make the hard decisions in life. It seemed natural to DeeDee, too. When she began maturing, she had wanted Dad to be there, when boys came by to pick her up for a date, to give them a stern look and some key advice. And later, when she walked down the aisle, she had wanted Dad at her side, patting her hand to calm her nerves.

It was not to be, of course. Two weeks after her twelfth birthday, it all came crashing down. A drunk smashed into his car as he drove home from work, killing him instantly. The grief was total, for both DeeDee and her mother. The shock and crying lasted for days. They couldn't function; her uncle had to come in and handle things.

Why did this have to happen to me?

DeeDee shook her head. She had gone from missing Stephen to missing her Dad, and neither one would help her get ready for her date with Carl. She dabbed her eyes again and forced herself to think about something else. Unbidden, her guilt surfaced. She remembered how she had treated her mother after her Dad's death. In her little prepubescent mind, events that occurred were somehow her mother's fault. Now, she knew she had just been lashing out and Mom had been the closest person to her.

They had long since made up. But for a few years, DeeDee had been a little hell-raiser.

Her mother had tried to be patient and understanding. Probably would've sent her to counseling if she could have afforded it. But after her father died, money became a big problem. He hadn't had much life insurance and when that ran out, her Mom had been forced to sell the house and move them into an apartment. DeeDee could remember thinking that her world had come to an end. First the loss of her father, then all her father's memories in their house. She had blamed her mother for that, too.

As she had developed into a young woman, DeeDee made her mother worry, perhaps as punishment. DeeDee had tried drugs and alcohol, but that didn't scratch the itch she felt, the emptiness caused by her father's death. It only masked it. For many, that would have been enough, but DeeDee kept looking.

She had found what she had been missing in sexual stimulation — including punishments — no doubt caused by her father's spankings. She was old enough now to know that she'd been sexually stimulated by his callused hand on her bottom. She sought out anything that would create that tingle in the stomach and loins. It made her feel whole again, if even just for a while.

It had started in high school, during her junior year. She'd had a crush on Rob Fisher, a handsome senior on the basketball team. When he'd hugged her, held her close, she could imagine it was Dad holding her, keeping her safe.

She'd lost her virginity to Rob on their second date, in the back of his mother's minivan that he'd borrowed. They'd told their parents they were going to the movies, then parked on the side of a remote road and made out. It was cramped and awkward in the back seat, but DeeDee couldn't stop herself, nor Rob. They didn't even remove all their clothes. In anticipation of the event, she'd worn a skirt that she simply flipped up out of the way. She let Rob remove her panties, that familiar tickling sensation filling her loins. She remembered being stunned by the size of his cock, even though it was of average size she later learned. It had just seemed too big to fit inside her.

She had hugged him fiercely, afraid to watch as he adjusted himself between her legs. When she felt her hymen tear, she cried, not because it hurt, but because the feelings she'd hoped for lasted just a moment. The anticipation of the event had been far better than the sex itself. Rob had climaxed quickly and it was over. She hadn't told him how empty she had suddenly felt.

When she had confided in her best friend, Lucy, about the night and her disappointment, Lucy had said that it was always that way the first time. She told her all about orgasms, something DeeDee had not fully understood before. "Just relax," Lucy had told her. "Try it again. You'll see."

But she hadn't seen. Rob tried to help her in his gentle but clumsy way, yet she never achieved that climax Lucy had described. They eventually broke up and DeeDee dated other boys and had sex with a few, but none could sustain that anticipation, that sexual stimulation she craved. They all wanted to fuck her quickly and didn't understand why she wanted to prolong the act.

She had discovered the answer herself, during the spring of her senior year. It had been a hot day, promising to hit eighty. DeeDee had been in her room, in a bad mood because she didn't have any clean panties. So, she'd gone without them. She wore baggy shorts, so it really didn't matter. No one would notice.

Yet the feeling she'd had, walking around campus, knowing that she was naked underneath her shorts, gave her a glimpse of what she'd been missing. She liked the feel of her naked sex, the cool air occasionally brushing her tuft of hair. It had made her wet. It had been such a simple thing too.

When she got home that afternoon, DeeDee had gone straight to her room and masturbated. She had her first real orgasm, more powerful than anything she'd felt with a boy. She had to bite her pillow to keep from screaming. *So that's what Lucy had been talking about*, she'd thought to herself.

When she recovered, she noticed her Mom had washed her clothes and left a laundry basket on her rug. She'd stared at the clean clothes for a minute, then carefully put everything away, including all her panties. Her mind whirled.

The next morning, after her shower, she had hesitated over the drawer, letting her fingers brush the silky garments. Then she closed it and went to the drawer containing her bras. Again she had hesitated, relishing the feeling in her stomach and loins, the tingle in her nipples. She remembered her orgasm and wanted to reach those heights again.

She had walked naked to her closet and chose a dark blue blouse—very concealing—and another pair of baggy shorts. DeeDee had felt delightfully naughty not to be wearing underwear. She doubted anyone could see, so she felt safe.

Of course the boys noticed—her nipples seemed to poke out all day. It only increased her sexual stimulation. She got lots of looks, a few comments. Even the male teachers suddenly wanted to talk to her about her assignments, up close, their eyes glancing down when they thought she wasn't looking.

For a few weeks, DeeDee was in heaven. She loved the feel of her nipples against her blouses or t-shirts, and the attention. Too soon, however, that began to pale. She felt she was losing her tingle, as she had called it. She believed it was because her baggy shorts too well concealed her secret. So one day, during late May, she'd worn a skirt to school without her panties.

This simple act had ratcheted up her libido tremendously. The feeling of her legs swishing under her skirt, her naked pussy open to the breeze, kept a smile on her face all day long. She had felt so very naughty she couldn't wait to get home and rub herself. She'd stopped off in the bathroom after fifth period, ready to relieve her itch, but there had been too many other girls present. She could only enter a stall, cup her mound and press her fingers hard against her clit, biting her lip to keep from causing a climax. God, she had been so close! That afternoon, as soon as she got home, she gave herself to two quick orgasms.

Remembering that day, and the days that followed, brought a smile to DeeDee's face for the first time. She peered into the mirror and finished putting on her makeup, wondering how her date with Carl might go.

Chapter Three

Seven o'clock sharp, Carl appeared at DeeDee's doorstep, freshly washed, shaved and dressed. He had never anticipated a date more than this one in many long years. His nerves jangled anew as he rang the doorbell.

DeeDee appeared in moments and took his breath away. She was wearing a full-length sleeveless peach-colored dress, belted in the middle, big buttons running all the way down. A pale yellow scarf helped conceal the scoop neck. Perhaps she was being modest. Her hair was done up in a bun and she had gold earrings in the shape of dolphins.

"My god, you look lovely," he said without thinking.

She blushed and it only flattered her features. She invited him in. Carl stumbled past her, thinking about how fortunate he was and what a complete jerk Frank had been to lose her.

"I'll be ready in a minute. I just have to finish up."

"Take your time. But keep in mind, if you're going to get any more beautiful, we're going to need a police escort."

She gave him a big smile and disappeared into the bathroom. Carl rearranged his pants, giving his cock a steely glare.

Timing is everything, mister!

When she came out a few minutes later, a whiff of perfume preceded her. Something expensive and very sexy. His cock throbbed with need.

"Would you like a drink before we go?"

Carl hesitated. He didn't want to drink much—he was afraid it might dull his enjoyment of this evening. Yet, he wanted to stay in her apartment alone with her just a few minutes longer.

"Sure. Just a quick one."

She turned to the kitchen and fixed two martinis on the rocks. He watched her work. He couldn't help but notice there didn't seem to be a panty line under the smooth curve of her dress. Nor did he see a bra strap up where her tanned shoulder disappeared into the dress. His cock noticed as well.

She came toward him, drinks in hand. Carl took one and gave a tentative sip. "Umm, perfect." He was talking about a lot more than the martini.

They stood there, drinking silently for a few minutes. Carl thought about safe topics, like the weather or the books she liked, but he really wondered if he dared to ask the pressing question on his mind. He feared scaring her off, yet his curiosity burned to know. Maybe it was the writer in him.

"DeeDee?" He jumped in without really thinking about it.

"Yes?" She looked at him over the rim of her glass, perfect lips leaving perfect pale red prints.

"I, um, couldn't help but notice... I don't mean to pry... I mean, I'm just curious..." Carl flailed about, wishing he'd kept his mouth shut.

Mirth flashed in her eyes. "You're wondering about my underwear—or lack of it, right?"

She had nailed him. "Well, yes. Forgive me for noticing. I hope I'm not—"

"It's okay." She waved a hand. "Most men notice. I guess I should be flattered by it. But the thing is, I just don't like to wear them. Never really have. My breasts aren't so big so that I need a bra and I find panties just pinch me or ride up." She laughed. "Maybe I should wear those big granny panties—what do you think?"

"Um." The mental image startled him. "Er, I can't see you in granny panties… I mean—"

She laughed again. That she would be so open and easy-going about it floored him. Carl thought he might be risking the goodwill he had built up by even mentioning it, but she talked about it as if he had asked about a book she was reading.

"Does it make you uncomfortable?"

His head shook firmly with each syllable. "Not. At. All. I find it incredibly sexy. How long has this been going on?"

A vacant look passed briefly over her face. It was just long enough for Carl to notice it. "Every since I was in high school. We lived in Texas and it was really hot much of the year. Somewhere about my senior year, I just took off the damn things and felt so much better, I never wanted to put them on again."

"Wow." He could imagine DeeDee as a teenager, driving the boys wild. "I'll bet you were popular."

That infectious laugh returned. "I suppose. I didn't do it to attract boys, but they certainly seemed to notice."

"If a girl had done that at my high school, I think I'd've spent a lot of time trying to figure out ways to look up her skirt."

"Oh, yeah, they tried. Fortunately, it was the last few weeks of school, so no one had time to get really excited."

"Did you go to college like that?"

Again, that vacant expression. As if a memory had overloaded her circuits. Then she nodded, an impish smile on her face.

"I'll bet your mother worried about you, didn't she?"

"Oh, yes. She was sure I'd turn up pregnant. I told her to relax, I knew what I was doing. God, I was such a little rebel!"

The story excited Carl. He could feel his cock responding. He thought he'd better get her out of the apartment soon or he'd be unable to resist the caveman desire to toss her onto the couch and fuck her brains out.

"Well, we'd better go." He took the final sip of his drink.

"Great." She rose in one fluid motion and smoothed down her dress. Carl opened the door and escorted her out. For the second time since he'd met her, he wished he had a nicer car to drive. At least it was clean—he'd seen to that. He opened the door and helped DeeDee in. He walked around to the driver's side, taking a moment to press one hand hard against his cock. *Later!* They headed downtown.

"Where are you taking me?"

How about a motel with a vibrating bed? "Café Biscotti. Have you ever eaten there?"

"Just once. I really liked it."

"Good."

They arrived in fifteen minutes and Carl parked in the lot behind the restaurant. They entered and Carl gave the maitre-d' his name.

"Oh, yes, Mr. Harman. Right this way, please."

They were escorted to a small table near the back, next to a fake ficus tree. The lighting was fashionably dim. They took their menus and studied them while Carl tried to think of something witty to say. He didn't want to come across as a sexist pig or a doofus.

"So, tell me about yourself." He smiled, hoping to disguise his nervousness.

"Not much to tell, really. Grew up in Texas, moved here to go to college — UCSB. Been here ever since."

"That's a long ways to go for college. What made you decide to come to California?"

"Oh, I suppose it was the freedom of really being on your own. Or maybe the ocean. I just had to get away."

Carl nodded. "I know that feeling." He found himself wondering again about DeeDee's clothing habits. "I'll bet you fit in well here."

"How do you mean?"

"Well, you know, Santa Barbara girls are probably freer about what they wear than in conservative Texas, aren't they?"

Her confused look flashed into understanding. "Oh, you mean…"

"Yeah."

She smiled. "You sure are interested in that."

"I can't help it. I think it's part of the male code of conduct. When confronted by a woman who doesn't wear underwear, find out as much as you can." He shrugged and dipped his head. "Maybe it's the writer in me."

"The writer?"

"Yeah. It makes me very curious, all the time. About everything."

"Those are pretty naughty thoughts, mister. I hope you're not planning to write about me." She said it teasingly, and Carl suspected she rather liked the idea.

He sipped his water, thinking. He would love to do a lot more than that. He felt his cock twitch again. "Only if you have a story to tell. Just about everyone has one. Tell me yours."

She shook her head. "Uh huh. I barely know you."

He tipped his head. "That's true. But now I know you have a story. Eventually, you'll have to tell me."

"Oh, really?"

"Yes. You will succumb to my charms." He said it in a self-deprecating way, even though he meant it. He shifted in his seat to give his cock more room.

The waiter came, and the moment was lost. They ordered dinner and chatted about ordinary things, as each tried to get to know the other better. But Carl could feel the undercurrent of sexual tension heavy in the air, like a gardenia on a warm spring evening. He wanted to know all of DeeDee's secrets. He also knew better than to push.

After dinner, they took a walk down to the beach where they both took off their shoes and let their toes dig into the sand. DeeDee teased him by twirling around. Her dress, buttoned down front as it was, didn't fly up, but it certainly did in his imagination.

He turned sideways and pulled on his pants, trying to keep from being pinched. *Jeez*, he thought, *this girl's gonna kill me. Death by blue balls.*

DeeDee apparently had spotted his actions, for she giggled and put one hand to her mouth in mock horror. "Am I making you uncomfortable?" she teased.

"Yeah, you could say that. But in a nice way."

"Is this all from my strange little habit?"

He nodded. Then he looked down at the bulging front of his pants and said, "Down, Simba!"

DeeDee collapsed into giggles.

* * * * *

DeeDee's attraction to Carl only grew the more she was with him. Their dinner had caused that familiar flutter in her stomach, just like she had felt with Stephen. She'd also felt it a little with Frank at first, so that was not the best indicator. Still, she found herself curious about Carl and what kind of man he really was, inside.

She'd already seen him under pressure and admired his control. Now she saw the playful side of him as they stood on the beach. He was not afraid of acting silly, yet he exuded a quiet strength.

She suddenly felt the urge to let him into her life more, just to see where this relationship might go. Was that too risky? She didn't care. After Frank, Carl had to be a step up.

She sat down suddenly, feeling the still-warm sand against the thin material of her dress. DeeDee kept her legs primly together and didn't object when Carl joined her and put his arm around her.

"Nice night," she said, for lack of anything else to say.

"Sure is." He squeezed her close. For a moment, DeeDee felt like she was back in the arms of Stephen. Carl exhibited the same kindness, the same strengths.

She turned her head away, surprised by the sudden onslaught of emotions.

"What's wrong?"

Of course he would notice—he was so wonderfully sensitive. "Oh, nothing. Just an old memory flashed up." She shook herself. "I'll be okay."

Carl put a finger along her chin and turned her toward him. She knew he could see the shiny wetness in her eyes.

"You're crying." He paused. "You must've really loved him."

Gawd! His accurate guess floored her. She felt a tear run down her cheek. She couldn't speak, she could only nod. For a moment, she wasn't sure if she was crying over Stephen or her father, both lost too young.

"What was his name?"

"S-Stephen." She didn't feel comfortable yet talking about her father.

"What happened to him?"

"He-he died. Last year."

Carl nodded, pursing his lips. He looked out at the ocean for a moment. Then he turned back. "I know it's painful, so I won't press you, but whenever you'd like to talk about him, I'd like to hear."

"Why? Most men don't want to hear about old lovers."

"I suspect this Stephen was different. You still hurt. Maybe by talking about it, I can help you ease the pain."

DeeDee shook her head. How could she share the secret life she'd had with Stephen? *Or should I say Master Stephen.*

She wanted to tell him. She longed to find a strong man who could understand the strange life she had led until so very recently. But few men could fathom it. Or they just took advantage of her submissive nature, like Frank.

"Come on, I'll take you home." Carl stood.

She looked up, disappointed that he hadn't pressed her. Then she gave him a shy smile as he helped her to her feet.

Chapter Four

Carl's mind worked overtime as he drove DeeDee home. There was something big she was keeping to herself. Probably because she had only just met him. She didn't trust him yet. No surprise. But he had to admit, he was very curious. Something about her relationship with this Stephen guy. He'd have to just wait and see if she would open up about it.

He pulled up outside her apartment complex, got out and opened her door. She seemed surprised at the courtesy. He held her hand as they walked to her door.

She unlocked it, before turning expectantly. Carl leaned in and kissed her gently on the lips. They were round and soft and delicious. He reached up and cupped her jaw, then kissed her again. He felt her press back against the doorjamb, abandoning herself in the kiss.

They broke apart and gazed into each other's eyes. "I had a great time with you tonight, DeeDee," he breathed. "I find you…fascinating."

She smiled. "That's just first-date lust talking," she teased.

He nodded. "Oh, yes, there's some of that. But there's more to it. I feel a strong attraction to you already, as if I've known you for longer than just a day." He winced inwardly at that trite statement, even though it was true.

Carl stepped back, wondering if he'd said too much. DeeDee stared at his eyes, as if judging him. She seemed to make a decision. "Would you like to come in for a nightcap? It's still early."

Oh, mamma!

"Yeah, I would." Carl felt his cock salute her invitation. He hoped he didn't appear too obvious. He worked hard to keep a lecherous leer from taking over his face.

They went inside. DeeDee carefully closed the door behind them. "Make yourself at home, I'll get the drinks." She disappeared into the kitchen.

Carl took the opportunity to give his pants a yank and mentally curse his erection. *Later, bub, later.* He walked to the bookshelf and grabbed the first book he found. Nothing like a boring text on women's lib to kill the hard-on.

He was surprised to see the book he held was Nancy Friday's "My Secret Garden." He'd heard of it—fantasies written for women, by women. Carl noticed a couple of dog-eared pages inside. He flipped to the first one and began to read.

As he did, his eyes opened wide. It was a masturbatory fantasy about a submissive woman and the actions she took at the behest of her master. Did women really fantasize about that? He knew men did. And why was it bookmarked? Did DeeDee—

"Here's—" DeeDee came in carrying the drinks, then stopped short when she spotted him reading the red-covered book.

Carl quickly put it back on the shelf as he hastily tried to act nonchalant. "Oh, hi." He could feel his cheeks redden. "I was just browsing." He desperately tried to think of something to say.

"You enjoy Nancy Friday's works?" DeeDee beat him to the punch.

"Uh, I haven't actually read it before. I'd heard of her, of course." He didn't know how much he should admit to. He couldn't very well tell her the truth, could he? *Sorry, I was just looking for a dull book to read in order to shrink my raging hard-on?*

She handed him a drink. "Tell me which story you were reading."

He stopped and caught the look in her eyes. It was a look of frank openness. He guessed that she was challenging him. *If you'll be honest, I'll be honest.*

"It was a story about a submissive woman," he said. "She was being made to walk out in public with very few clothes on."

She tipped her head. "And why did you happen to read that one?"

"It was bookmarked. I'm guessing it's one of your favorites."

She flashed him a sly grin. "Perhaps."

"Is that what Stephen did for you?"

Now it was her turn to be honest, he thought. "You really are curious about him, aren't you?"

"Oh, yes. But not if it's too painful. I'm only talking about the good parts."

She stared into her martini glass. "I-I haven't…told anyone before."

Now Carl was sure he wanted to hear it. She had piqued his writer's curiosity. He sat down on the couch and indicated she should sit in the upholstered chair opposite. "I would really like to hear it, DeeDee. Will you tell me?"

She nodded and her face got a vacant, dreamy look to it. She started out hesitantly, then gathered steam as the story unfolded.

"My first year in college. Stephen...was my English professor. Stephen J. Evers. He was a nice-looking, slightly balding, middle-aged man...who always seemed so...proper. I was still rebelling, even though I was away from my mother. I still didn't want to wear underwear.

"One day, he called me into his office. He told me he could tell I wasn't wearing a bra and that it was distracting to the other students. He'd make me sit in one of those wooden school chairs while he...walked around me, talking about my...habit, telling me I should be more discreet. All the while, I could feel his eyes on my knees, as if he was trying to see up past the hem of my dress. Or on my...breasts, though he couldn't see anything through my blouse."

Carl was rapt with attention. His drink remained forgotten in his hand. His cock re-awoke and trumpeted its presence.

"The first time, he threatened to call my mother if I kept it up. That was almost laughable—it wasn't much of a threat. She never could stop me from doing it.

"At the same time, I didn't want to go back to wearing panties and bras, so I told him how hot and uncomfortable they made me. I mean, he really didn't have any leverage over me. He couldn't flunk me just because of what I wore. Yet, it made me...excited. Then...I don't know why I did it, just intuition, I guess. I spread my knees apart a little and eased the skirt up just a bit, showing my knees. He licked his lips and told me I'd have to report to him regularly if I kept ignoring the rules. I could've said no, I don't have to and that would've been the end of it, but I played along. I told him I'd rather do that than put on the damn things, so we…came to sort of an arrangement."

"You'd continue to tease him and he wouldn't tell you to wear underclothes in his class."

"Right."

"Was he satisfied just to see your knees?"

She blushed pink. "No. Each time I went to see him, he wanted to push it a little further. He never told me to do it in so many words, he just kept up with these empty threats to call my mom or to report me unless I agreed to wear undergarments, unless…"

She sat motionless in the chair, her face blank, her mind completely occupied with her story. Carl was equally rapt with attention.

"I got the hint. I'd unbutton the top button of my blouse and ease my skirt up, just a little. He'd stop talking and just breathe a little more heavily. We'd just stay there like that for a few minutes, then he'd let me go. The next time, he'd start again. Each time, pushing it a little further."

Carl's cock ached for release. This was the best story he'd heard in years. His future bestseller was writing itself in his head. It might even be banned in Boston. That was, if DeeDee allowed him to use her story.

"You could've reported him, you know. I mean, the professors aren't supposed to fool around with the students." Carl thought the man was risking a lot.

"I know. But that was the last thing I wanted to do. It made me…very excited."

Carl knew exactly what she meant. Just like the fantasy she'd bookmarked. Someday, he'd have to read the whole damn story. But right now, this was far better.

"So you used him, just as much as he used you."

She made a face. "Well, if you put it that way, I guess so. We really were just teasing each other. He tried to keep his distance, you know, to be professional."

Carl knew that couldn't last. "So, you kept going to his office?"

"Yes. It was so…n-n-naughty." The word seemed to catch in her throat.

He saw the color rise in her cheekbones. Her eyes dilated as she remembered those days.

"Show me what you were doing, at first." He honestly didn't know where that came from. It wasn't even a question, it was a demand. A soft demand, but still a demand.

She widened her eyes, then put her drink down and cupped the hem of her dress with two delicate hands. She pulled it up over her knees. "It was about like this, at first," her voice shook a little.

"And the top?"

She left the dress where it was and reached up to the big buttons on her chest. Carl could see her hands trembling. He almost told her to stop, but his words caught in his throat. She unbuttoned the top button underneath the scarf.

That scarf would have to go, he decided.

"How long did this go on?"

"Oh, months. That entire semester."

"I imagine you were showing him quite a bit by the time you left his class. Show me how it progressed."

His own boldness startled him. She didn't seem panicked by it. If anything, it was turning her on as well, he could tell. She let her hands drift to the hem and she pulled it to mid-thigh. Then she unbuttoned another button.

"This was about how it was about mid-term," she said, her face dreamy, remembering. "It started out real slow. He'd call me in once a week or so. He would stand up and look down my blouse. I doubt he could've seen much. But I could see the erection in his pants right in front of my face."

"He was a very patient man," Carl commented.

"Yes, he was. At the time, it was about all I could handle. I think he knew that. He didn't want to risk his tenure. If he pushed me too far, I might flee and report him. I think he had more to lose than I did."

"But you didn't because you liked it?"

"Yesss." She drew out the word.

"You like to tease, don't you?"

"Can't you tell?" She smiled at him. Sitting there, with her dress halfway up her thighs, her top unbuttoned, Carl could imagine the effect she had on the horny professor.

"Go on. Show me what happened next."

She sighed, a lovely, sexy sigh. "You're a...a n-naughty man, Carl." Odd. That adjective seemed to catch in her throat. "Later, he made me spread my legs apart more."

"Like this?" He moved closer and eased her knees about eight inches apart.

"Yesss," she hissed, remembering.

"How far up did he make you pull your skirt?"

"Practically all the way. I'm sure he could just about see me...my..."

"What? Say it."

"You know."

"You have to tell me."

She looked away. Her voice was soft. "V-vagina."

Carl wondered if the professor would've let her off so easily. "Come on—is that what you called it when you were with him?"

"I-I tried to."

He was beginning to get an inkling of the hold Evers had on her. "But Stephen didn't let you, did he?"

She shook her head.

"What did he make you call it? Tell me."

"P-p-pussy."

"Say the whole sentence."

"I-I'm sure he could almost see m-my p-pussy."

"Did he touch you?"

"Not then." She shook her head firmly. "Not while I was still in his class. He'd just look at me and make me show him a little more each time. By the end of the semester, he'd had me unbutton most of the buttons on my blouse and pull my skirt up to...um, right there."

"Where?"

She sighed, but then continued. "So the hem was right at m-my p-pussy."

DeeDee gave a slight shudder. "You know, I can remember thinking how much sexual power I had as a teenager, but later, the power seemed to shift. It was like it had me."

"What happened after you left his class?"

"Nothing happened. I didn't see him that spring. Summer came. I got a job, worked a lot. Moved from the dorms into a small apartment that I shared with another girl. But I never stopped thinking about him. For a few months that fall, I tried to move on, just to forget about it. I dated some, but they all seemed so immature.

"Then, one day, I just showed up at his office, when I knew he'd be there. I knocked on his door and when he said, 'Enter,' I felt this little thrill throughout my body. He seemed surprised to see me. Surprised, but glad."

"I'll bet you picked up where you left off."

She nodded. "I was drawn to him. It may seem surprising to you now, but I really looked forward to it. It was the sexiest thing I'd ever done."

"You weren't having sex with any of the college boys?"

She shrugged. "Oh, yes. Now and again. Nothing serious. They seemed so juvenile compared to Stephen."

Carl gave a short laugh. "I can understand that. He was patient, while boys that age probably just wanted to get on with it."

"That's true. I liked the game, you see. I liked the way he made me feel."

"So what would happen, during those sessions?"

"More of the same. We picked right up where we left off."

"Show me. But first, take off your scarf."

A small smile moved across her face. She untied the scarf and let it fall away. Now he could easily see the two loose buttons and the expanse of neck above. Her cleavage showed between the opening.

He nodded at her. She pulled the dress up even higher now, to the V of her legs. With her legs apart, Carl could see the first pale edge of flesh. He found it difficult to breathe. She reached up and unfastened another button. "This was how it was early in my sophomore year...I was practically exposed."

"How did it make you feel?"

"I can remember it turning me on so powerfully that afterwards, I had to go back to my apartment and, you know..."

"What? Stephen would want you to say it."

"...masturbate."

"Is it turning you on now?" He already knew the answer.

"Y-yes." Her voice was pitched low.

"Didn't you ever wear jeans or shorts, like most college girls?"

"Yes, but not on the days I visited Stephen. He...he wouldn't let me. Only skirts."

Carl stood and moved up over her, looking down her dress to see the curve of her breasts. He still couldn't see her nipples. His throbbing cock was just inches from her face. She stared at it for a moment then closed her eyes. He could see a sheen of sweat forming on her forehead.

He stepped back and with great effort, sat down, adjusting his cock in his slacks. He took another sip of his drink. "What happened next?"

DeeDee opened her eyes. "He asked me to pull my dress up farther, past my…well, you know."

"Tell me. Tell me just what he said."

She let out a breath. "I've never told anybody this. He said, 'Pull your dress up past your pussy, my dear, sweet, naughty girl'."

"Did you?"

"Yesss."

"Show me."

As if hypnotized, she closed her eyes and pulled her dress up until he could see all of her sex. She shaved down there, he noticed immediately. The skin was smooth and lightly tanned, so she must lie out in the sun naked part of the time.

"And your blouse?"

She left the dress in place and began to fumble with the one button remaining near her belt. "He said he wanted all the buttons loose. I can still hear him, 'All the buttons, my naughty girl, that's right. This is what happens to girls who refuse to wear underwear.'"

"Did he touch you then?"

"Not at first. He'd just stand over me and look. I usually kept my eyes closed, or else I'd be looking right at his crotch."

Carl stood again and moved in close. He could smell her strong sexual odor, a sweet scent of honey and musk. Looking down, he could see her juices were oozing out and coating her labia, which had visibly swelled.

"What happened next?"

"He b-began asking me to come by more often. I was happy to, let me tell you. I'm sure everyone thought I was a very n-n-naughty girl, having to report to the professor so often."

There was her trouble with that word again. "Is that what he called you, his naughty girl?"

"Yes, at…at first."

Carl remained close to her. Looking down, he could see her nipples now and watched the rise and fall of her breasts as she breathed. He sensed she needed a little push to tell the next part.

"What would he do?"

Her voice caught, then her words came quickly: "He'd, um, touch himself, through his clothes. He'd make me watch. I tried to close my eyes, but he wouldn't let me. 'Look, my dear, sweet child,' he'd say. 'Naughty girls must see what awaits them.' It was a role he was playing, and I loved it."

DeeDee opened her eyes and looked up at Carl. She was nineteen again, sitting below Evers, feeling the sexual heat and embarrassment, all rolled up into one.

"He asked me to open my legs…wider so he could stand closer," she continued, another hitch in her voice.

Carl moved closer until his knees touched hers. Without a word, she opened her legs, allowing him to edge nearer. His cock actually hurt now, so he unbuttoned his pants to give it a little slack.

Her eyes opened wide at that. "He did that too," she said. "He'd loosen his pants, then begin to rub himself from the outside."

Carl mimicked the actions of the professor, letting his fingers stroke his hard cock. She closed her eyes again and he said at once, "Look, my dear, sweet child. Naughty girls must see what awaits them."

Her eyes fluttered open. Her mouth was agape. She seemed to have trouble breathing.

"Then what happened?"

"He told me to start meeting him late on Fridays, because the students and the teachers always left quickly after the last class," she said softly. "He'd lock his office door." She stopped. Carl had to prompt her to continue.

"Things…things seemed to accelerate after that. He'd tell me to unbutton my blouse and pull it away from my breasts. And I had to lift up my skirt all the way and sit bare-assed on the chair."

"Do it."

She obeyed as best she could with the full dress on. She unbuttoned the last of the large buttons below her belt so she could fold the material back out of the way. Next, she unfastened the belt and let it drop to the floor. Now the dress hung open all the way down.

She tried to stand, but Carl was too close. He had to move back to give her room. She stood and swept the dress behind her, exposing her beautifully smooth sex and shapely hips. Her nipples stood erect from her breasts. As soon as she sat down again, he moved back between her legs. She never tried to close them.

"Then what?"

"He'd…he'd touch my breasts," she said so softly Carl had to lean down to hear her.

"What? Speak up."

"He'd touch my breasts," she said louder. He could see the blush in her neck and cheeks.

"Like this?" he asked, stroking her gently. Her nipples seemed to grow even harder.

She nodded, her eyes closed again, apparently reliving the past.

"What did he do with his cock?"

She turned away for a moment and bit her lip. "He…he took it out and showed me."

Carl unzipped his pants and let his engorged cock spring free. "Look at it." Her eyes fluttered open again and he heard a tiny gasp. "Then what?"

"He'd make me look at it while he…he rubbed it."

"What did he say?"

She shuddered slightly. "He said, 'Look at what naughty girls do to men'."

Carl began to stroke his hard member, just inches from her face. "Did he come?"

She only nodded silently, her eyes wide.

"What would happen when he came?"

She murmured something indistinct.

"He would come on your face?" he pressed.

The word was torn from her. "Yesss."

"Then watch."

She kept her eyes open as he masturbated. It didn't take too long. She had a powerful effect on Carl. He spasmed and ropy streams of sperm squirted across her lips, cheek and nose. She blinked but said nothing until he prompted her.

"Now what would he do?"

"He…he had a mirror on his desk. He'd pick it up and show me the s-sperm on my face. He'd say: 'This is what happens to naughty girls who don't wear underwear.

Look at my s-sperm all over your face. You are a Naughty Girl, aren't you?' He'd make me say it."

"Do you have a hand mirror?"

She nodded, the white sperm a contrast against her tanned face.

"Go get it." He stepped back. He was beginning to feel the power Evers had over her and he couldn't help but wield it. Just for a little while, he told himself. She likes it so.

She rose, the dress flapping open as she disappeared into the bathroom. She returned a moment later with the small mirror. Carl took it from her and motioned for her to sit again. She moved the dress out of the way and sat, her legs apart. He moved closer.

He held the mirror out so she could see her face. "Say it."

"I-I'm a Naughty Girl."

"Only I'll bet he didn't call it 'sperm,' did he?"

Her eyes grew wide. She just shook her head.

"What did he say?"

"C-c-cum."

"What? I can't hear you."

"Cum."

"Let's use the right words, okay? Then what?"

"He told me to lick the cum off my lips. I didn't want to at first. Th-this is when the power seemed to shift from me to him, but in a good way. It was as if I didn't want to refuse him. So…so I did what he said."

"Do it."

She licked the pearly substance from around her lips. Carl could tell she liked it. The rest of it remained on her face.

"What about the rest?"

"At first, he'd clean it off with a tissue. Later, he'd make me scoop it up with my finger and swallow it."

"Go on," he told her. "Just like you did for Evers."

She ran her finger over her skin. Carl held up the mirror, letting her see the smeared gobs of cum across her face. "Do you feel like a naughty girl again?"

She nodded.

"What? I can't hear you."

"Yes, I'm a Naughty Girl."

"He didn't stop there, did he?"

"Nooo. I think I could've stopped it at any time. Part of me wanted to. Part of me didn't. He'd tell me, after our session on Friday, that if I ever wanted to stop I could simply by wearing a bra and panties the next time."

"Did you?"

She shook her head. "No, I didn't. When I showed up again, he'd act disappointed in me, but I knew he was pleased."

"And you kept going to him."

"Yes, it was like I'd taken a powerful drug. No one had made me feel like that before."

"What happened next?" Carl absently rubbed his soft cock, encouraging it to grow hard again.

"He surprised me the next Friday. He told me he figured out why I didn't get embarrassed when I didn't wear panties."

"Oh?"

Her face flushed anew. Carl could tell this was an exciting new chapter of the story. His cock swelled. Her eyes fixated on it, just a few inches away.

"He…he said it was because of my…my, um, hair down there. 'It covers you up,' he told me. 'Naughty Girl thinks she's still good if her hair covers her pussy'. That was the first time he touched me, down there."

Carl interrupted. "No, he'd want you to say it each time."

"My…my pussy. That was the first time he touched my pussy. He just grabbed a little pinch of hair and tugged on it. That was all. I was shocked, but it felt good too. He was wrong, of course. That wasn't the reason I didn't like panties. But he wouldn't listen. He…he told me to shave it off. I told him I couldn't. He said, 'Either shave it or come to my office next week wearing a bra and panties'. "

"What did you do?"

"I was fully prepared to wear underwear, just to show him up. I thought I should put a halt to our little games. It didn't seem right. But…but I didn't. I don't know why. I felt compelled somehow. Friday morning, when I took a shower and shaved my legs, I-I j-just kept going."

"How did it feel?"

"Like I was really naked for the first time. In that, he'd been right."

"Is that why you keep it smooth, even today?"

She nodded, her face suffused in pink.

"What did he say during the next visit?"

"He took me into his office and closed the door. 'Show me', was all he said. I lifted my skirt up until he could see me. He...he touched it—my...my pussy, rubbing his fingers over the smoothness. He made me spread my legs apart. He found a few areas of stubble, places I couldn't reach very well. He made a tsking sound and told me I'd have to do a better job."

"Did he make you come?"

"No, and I really wanted him to. Just being exposed like that, well, it kept me on edge. He came on my face again. I went home immediately and masturbated. I was so hot. I imagined it was him...touching me."

"So during your next visit..." Carl felt in a rush to find out the rest.

"I went to his office. He told me to remove all my clothes. 'Naughty sluts don't need clothes. They like to be naked for their masters'. That was the first time he called me a slut and him the master. Soon that became his name for me."

"Naughty Slut?"

"Yes."

"What did you think about it?"

"I don't know. I was all confused. But it made me tingle inside."

"Did you obey?"

"Yes. I was conditioned by this time. Besides, he'd seen me pretty much naked for months by then. So I got naked—even took off my shoes and socks—and he sat me on the chair again. He forced my legs apart and stood close. This part was, at least, familiar. He took out his cock and began to stroke himself. I waited, eyes opened, for the sperm bath, as usual. But just before he came, he ordered me to open my mouth—wide. I was shocked, but I did as he asked. He reached over with his left hand and grabbed the hand mirror and showed me. 'This is the face of a Naughty Slut, awaiting precious cum from her Master.' I could see myself clearly, mouth open, his cock poised just about an inch away, fluid oozing from the tip.

"Then he came and shoved his cock into my mouth. It wasn't too far in, but I nearly gagged just the same. I tried to pull away, but he just reached around with his right hand and held the back of my head. All the while, he kept the mirror steady in his left hand, aimed so I could see. 'Look at the Naughty Slut', he said. 'That's what you've become—a Naughty Slut.'"

Carl's cock was hard. But he didn't want to beat off again. He had a feeling this story went a lot further.

DeeDee continued: "I could taste the cum in my mouth. I had tasted it before, of course, but not very often. It tasted a little bitter. Then, just when I was trying to decide if I should spit it out or swallow it, he leaned down close to me and said, 'Swallow it. Naughty Sluts always swallow their Master's seed.' Then he reached down with his right hand and pressed the pads of three fingers hard against my clit.

"I came immediately. It was so powerful, I nearly fainted. And I swallowed all that cum. He knew what he was doing—he made me associate an earth-shattering orgasm with the taste of him. Suddenly, it no longer seemed bitter."

She eyed Carl's cock, just inches away. She could see the fluid on the tip.

"Did that become a regular part of the Friday sessions?"

"Yes, and I-I really liked it. Maybe it was like that first hit of heroin, not that I've ever tried it. But you know you need it after that. I needed Mast—I mean Stephen."

"It's all right, call him Master. It's part of the story, isn't it?"

She blushed. "Yes. And that's not all. He wouldn't let me say 'I' anymore. I had to say, 'Naughty Slut' when referring to myself. I'd show up on Friday and have to say, 'Naughty Slut is here, Master,' and later, 'Naughty Slut is naked for you, Master,' and finally, 'Naughty Slut wants your cum, Master.' I really started thinking of myself as a slut." She looked down. Her voice was merely a whisper. "And I liked it."

"What did he make you do next?" Carl rubbed his semi-hard cock gently. Her eyes came back up and she seemed riveted by it.

"He said I wasn't being punished enough for being a Naughty Slut. Th-that's when the, uh, spankings started."

"Spankings?"

"Yes. Oh, it wasn't much, really. Just part of my, um, training. He had these wooden rulers in his desk drawer—maybe a dozen of them. He'd tell me that I hadn't learned my lesson, that I was enjoying myself too much. He made me strip, then bend over the back of the chair and grip the seat."

This was something Carl could do, too. "Show me. Bring a chair from the kitchen." He stepped aside.

She stood in one fluid motion and moved away. Her face held a blank expression. She was back in the past, obeying Stephen. DeeDee returned with a chair and placed it in the middle of the room.

"You don't need that dress any longer," he told her. "Naughty Sluts don't wear clothes."

She seemed surprised that she still had it on, draped over her shoulders. She shrugged out of it then leaned over the chair. Her fingers gripped the seat.

"Continue your story," Carl told her, coming close to fondle her naked ass.

"The rulers hurt. They left a red mark."

"Like this?" he slapped her sharply. He could see his handprint turn from white to red.

"Yes," she squeaked, "only more concentrated in one spot."

"We'll have to get a ruler then."

"There's one in the desk drawer, over by the wall."

Carl started for it, then stopped. "Naughty Slut, go get Master the ruler for your punishment."

When she stood up, her eyes were round as the bottom of shot glasses. She went to the desk without a word and brought back a wooden ruler—probably just like the ones Evers had used on her. Why else would she have them to this day?

He nodded and she returned to her position, ass in the air, the back of the chair pressing into her stomach.

"Tell me what he'd say," he ordered.

She hesitated. Carl gave her a little slap with the end of the ruler. It left a nice mark that faded into pink.

She stared again in a rush. "He said I had not yet achieved total obedience. He started out with just four strokes, two on each cheek, but told me I would probably need more as time went on."

He gave her a good rap on her upper right cheek. She squealed. "Did Master allow you to squeal like that?"

"No, sir."

"Good, then take your punishment like a Naughty Slut." Carl cracked her across the other cheek. She jumped but made no sound. Nodding, he hit her on the right cheek again, just below the previous mark. She wiggled her ass at him. He landed the final blow. He could see the wetness oozing from her slit. This had turned her on tremendously.

"It's making you wet," he commented. "Did Master notice as well?"

She nodded. "He said he expected as much, since I was such a slut."

"What would he do after the spanking?"

She looked coy and bit her lip. "That was the first time he...he fucked me."

"Tell me about it."

"He bent me over the chair and made me spread my legs. He put his fingers into me, making me wetter. So he stood behind me—"

Carl moved behind her.

"—and grabbed the mirror and held it up at an angle so I could see his cock going into my p-pussy. He made me crane my neck back to watch him. He put his cock into me and started to rub me, inside."

Carl put his cock into her, just the tip, and let the bulbous head stroke her clit and G-spot. This was his second date with DeeDee and already he was fucking her, just like Evers did, all those years ago.

She began to have trouble speaking. Carl gave her a little slap on the ass with the ruler and told her to continue.

"He…he started out slowly. It drove me crazy. He kept telling me…to look back at the mirror, but it was hard to see. It was hard to…concentrate, too."

Carl continued stroking, trying to keep just the tip of his cock in her.

"He got excited and began to push harder until he was all the way in. He said, 'Naughty Slut, this is what happens to when you wiggle your naked ass at men. Naughty Sluts want to fuck.'"

Carl's cock was fully in her now. He leaned down and whispered, "Naughty Slut. Feel your Master's cock, Naughty Slut."

She gasped and hung her head down, rotating her hips to meet his thrusts. But Carl wanted to hear more. "Keep talking," he said.

"He…asked if I was on the pill. I said no—all my other lovers had used condoms. He didn't want to get me pregnant, so he stopped just before he came. He grabbed me by the shoulder…and spun me around, pushing me to my knees then he forced his cock into my mouth. It was already spurting. I could taste myself on him. I hadn't come yet, either, but he knew that. After he came in my mouth, he reached down and pressed one hand against my clit and rubbed it. I came in a big rush, like being on a roller coaster."

"Are you protected now? I want to come inside you." He didn't want to force her. He hadn't used a condom and suddenly felt guilty.

"P-please, M-M-Master."

Carl pressed in farther and brought his right hand around to her clit. He loved the smell of her, the shape of her body against his. As he stroked, nearing his release, he rubbed her clit vigorously. He wanted her to enjoy this as much as he did. She pressed back against him, her voice rising in octaves, then shuddered and orgasmed, hard, just as he released a flood of his seed into her.

It was a few minutes before either of them could speak.

Finally, Carl pulled away. His cock was soft. Fluids gushed from her slit. DeeDee had her head hanging low over the chair. Her hair was damp at the edges. He leaned down, putting his hand on her back.

"Did he fuck you every week from then on?"

She nodded without raising her head.

"He didn't get you pregnant?"

"No," she croaked softly. "He told me Naughty Sluts go on the pill. He gave me the address of the clinic and told me to have pills by the next week."

"Did you get them?"

"No…not at first. I was scared." She turned her face sideways so she could see him. "He got really mad the next Friday. He said, 'I told you, Naughty Sluts are on the pill. They have to be ready for their Master's cock at any time. That's why they don't wear panties. Don't you see?' I saw, all right, I was just scared.

"He spanked me a lot that day. I couldn't sit down after that, so he made me kneel in front of him and suck him until he came. 'Next week, you'd better have pills to show me or I'm going to spank you harder,' he said. 'And I'll fuck you anyway.'"

"Did you get them?"

"Yes, I did. But the nurse told me I'd have to time them to the beginning of my period, which, ironically, started Wednesday of that week. I went to him on Friday and said I had the pills, but I couldn't fuck him—"

"You used that word, 'fuck'?"

"Yes, Master always wanted me to use the crudest words."

"But you didn't say, '*I* couldn't fuck him,' did you?"

"Um, no. I said, 'Naughty Slut can't fuck you because she's having her period'."

"What did he say when you told him?"

"He said, 'Naughty Sluts never tell their Masters no. Naughty Sluts always seek to please them. You'll have to be punished for that.' He gave me six strokes with the ruler and told me if I ever said 'no' to him again, he would double it. Then he went to his drawer and got something out and handed it to me. It was a tube of KY Jelly."

"Did you know what it was for?"

"Yes, but I'd never done that before. I guess I'd lived a sheltered life."

"Were you scared?"

"Oh, yes, very much. But at least I knew I couldn't get pregnant. So he got himself all slippery, then had me lie on the couch, with my knees tucked up under me, my head down. I could feel him there, spreading more jelly around and in my asshole. He used his fingers to open me up. 'Master,' I said, 'will it hurt Naughty Slut?' He said, 'Maybe a little at first until my little slut gets stretched out. But that's what Naughty Sluts are for.'"

"How did it feel?"

"Oh, it hurt at first, just like he said. His cock felt enormous, going in. But he kept telling me to relax my muscles there and it got a little easier. Then he started stroking in earnest and it actually started to feel good. And when he reached around underneath me to rub my clit, it felt very good. When he came, I came too."

"Did you fuck that way often?"

"No. He actually preferred the regular way, except when I was having my periods."

"Did he fuck you the next week?"

"Oh, yes. I had barely started the pills and didn't know that they really don't take effect for a couple of weeks, at least. Master didn't tell me, either, though he had to know. He just said, 'My Naughty Slut is finally ready. This is the final lesson in being a whore.'"

"Wow." Carl couldn't think of anything else to say.

"Yeah. He had me believing it. He made me lie on the couch, on my back and he began to lick my pussy with his tongue. God, it was incredible! I'd never felt anything like it. He made me come two or three times.

"Then he crawled up over me and said, 'Look, Naughty Slut at your life from now on. To be used by your Master in every orifice whenever he needs a release. Your pleasures don't matter. They are secondary to mine.' Then he stuck his cock into me and fucked me."

Carl stuck his semi-hard cock into her and fucked her. This was no lovemaking, this was a man taking a woman, and the woman abandoning herself to the act of being conquered. Carl had never in his life felt such power over a woman. Even in the midst of the act, part of his mind told him he shouldn't be taking advantage of her like this, but that small voice was drowned out by the sheer pleasure of their coupling.

She was an energetic lover, no doubt driven by her memories of being under the control of her professor. Carl loved the way she writhed under him, clinging to his arms as if she were drowning, her head thrown back, her mouth agape in need. They rode together in careless abandon and when he came, they hugged each other like shipwreck survivors.

After a few minutes, Carl pulled up to look into her face. "How many times did you make love to him before you graduated from college?"

"Many times," she whispered. "Many, many times."

"Always at his office?"

She shook her head.

"How? Where?"

"At his house. He was divorced. He had an adult son, who lived in another city, so we had the place to ourselves."

"How would he contact you?"

"He wouldn't, really. I mean, he'd never call my apartment. We were still a big secret, you see. He ordered me to drive by every Saturday. When he wanted to see me, he'd hang a wooden red 'S' — for 'Slut' of course — on one of his porch posts. Then I'd come in through the back door and remove my clothes, ready for whatever games he had in mind."

"Why did you continue to do it?"

She smiled. "Because I loved him. And he gave me the greatest orgasms I've ever had."

"You liked being a slut for him?"

"Yes. Very much."

"And now he's gone?"

"Yes, he died last year of a heart attack. It was quite sudden. He was only fifty-eight."

"So you really miss him and his games."

She nodded, unable to speak.

Carl waited a moment. Then he lifted her chin gently with his fingers. "My Naughty Slut shouldn't cry. Master Carl will make her feel better."

Chapter Five

DeeDee closed the door behind Carl, stunned by how quickly events had developed. Carl had wanted to spend the night, but she insisted that he go, so she could sort out her feelings.

On the one hand, she felt some shame that she'd so easily succumbed to her darker desires and told Carl her story. On the other hand, she'd wanted him to know. She could tell, even in this short time, that Carl was a special man. He might not be as strong as Stephen had been, but he was kind and gentle and she believed he had her best interests at heart.

Now that she'd let her secret out, would that change their relationship? She knew it would. By telling Carl she enjoyed being submissive, she was opening herself up to a new dynamic in the man-woman interaction—one that she could no longer fully control.

How did she feel about that? It was hard to sort out. In many ways, it was similar to the feelings she'd had for Stephen. God, did he make her hot and wet! She realized just how much she had missed him. That's why she'd been so reckless in telling Carl about her past. Even Frank hadn't been privy to that secret, and she'd dated him for four months. Yet she had known, even on the first date with Frank, that he wasn't the man to entrust with that knowledge. She should've cut off the relationship earlier, but Frank was a hard man to shake. She smiled, remembering some of his good qualities. He did know how to make love to a woman.

Now she'd let Carl right into her soul. Just like that, on their second date! What if he turned out to be abusive or crazy? She didn't think he was, but she could be wrong.

"Aww, Master, why did you have to leave me?" she said to the ceiling. She wished she could talk to him for a few minutes, just long enough for him to reassure her that she'd done the right thing. He'd know, even if she didn't.

The irony was that she longed to give herself totally to another man. No one came close. Before Frank, there'd been a brief fling with Charlie, but he'd been far too selfish to stay with for long. Yet even then, she could recall wanting to tell him about Stephen, about her life with him, how much he had meant to her, what kind of games they had played. Caution had stilled her tongue. And it had served her well. Neither Charlie nor Frank would've been able to handle it. They would've used her submissiveness against her.

What would Carl do? Would he give her the same intense, electric feelings she'd had from Stephen? Would he tease her into powerful orgasms, make her shudder with relief, cry with joy? Or would he go too far, make her regret her indiscretion?

"Well, the cat's out of the bag now," she said to her dead lover, "so we'll just see what happens."

With that, DeeDee went to bed and fell asleep instantly, exhausted and, for the first time in months, completely satisfied.

She awoke to the telephone. She checked the clock. Eight-fifteen. That surprised her—she usually didn't sleep so late. Then she smiled, remembering why she had slept so soundly.

She reached for the phone. "Hello?"

"DeeDee?" It was Carl.

She felt a bit lightheaded. "Hi, Carl. You're calling early."

"I wanted to call and let you know how much I enjoyed our date last night…"

DeeDee felt a flush in her cheeks. She didn't know quite how to respond.

"…and to let you know, I understand that this all happened rather suddenly. Maybe you're having some doubts about me, or about what my intentions are. I thought I'd take you to lunch so we could talk about it."

DeeDee flopped back on her pillow and held a hand to her head. *Jeez! Is this guy for real? That's so sweet!*

"Well, sure. But I thought you had to work."

"I do. I'm working now. But I always have time for lunch."

"Okay."

"Great. I'll come by and pick you up at noon."

"Wait. Carl, rather than drive me to some restaurant where we'll have to speak in whispers, why don't I just fix you a sandwich here and we can talk?"

"Are you sure? That'd be great. I'll see you soon."

She hung up, surprised at how rapidly her heart was beating. She didn't know if it was a reaction to his kindness or just from hearing his voice. She rubbed her thighs together, delighting in the slippery sensations it created. God, he'd made her wet with just a handful of words. What was she going to be like when he came over?

"I'll be a horny mess," she said aloud, then giggled. She got up and headed for the shower.

Right at noon, the doorbell rang. DeeDee checked herself in the mirror one last time. She had on a t-shirt and shorts—no underwear, of course. She noticed how her nipples pressed hard against her shirt. She could feel herself getting wet again. *Calm down, girl!* She made sure her makeup was in place then went to the door.

Her heart fluttered when she saw Carl again, dressed for work in slacks and a blue shirt. *Don't be a schoolgirl!*

"Hi. Come on in."

He entered awkwardly. He didn't seem to know if he should kiss her or rip off her clothes and ravish her. She wasn't sure what she wanted either. Her body told a different story. It vibrated in his presence.

Finally, he leaned in and kissed her. She met his lips hungrily, giving him encouragement. After several seconds, he pulled back. She glanced down and was pleased to see the bulge in his pants. He seemed as awkward as a nerd at the prom.

"I've got lunch all ready. Come on into the kitchen." She led the way.

The kitchen was immaculate. Two plates with sandwiches were set up on the small table.

"Hope you like tunafish," she said, trying to ease the tension—sexual and otherwise—that permeated the air between them. "It's all I had."

"Tunafish is great. I love tunafish." He quickly sat down and DeeDee suspected he was trying to hide his erection. Whatever for?

"What would you like to drink? I have iced tea, beer, water…"

"Iced tea would be fine."

She poured them each a glass, then sat down across from him. He picked up a sandwich and took a small bite. "Delicious."

She waited. She almost enjoyed his discomfort. It made her believe he really cared about her feelings. Which was funny, because just seeing him here again made her want a repeat of last night. She wanted him to be in charge.

"Um, I thought we should talk about last night."

"Yes?" She batted her eyes innocently.

"Well, I wanted to make sure you felt okay about it. You know, it was kinda intense."

DeeDee smiled. Yes, it certainly was that. She wanted to make him feel better about it. She put a hand on his arm. "It's all right, Carl. I know what you're feeling today. I felt it too. I haven't felt that way since Stephen died."

"Really? That's good, isn't it?" He paused then frowned. "I mean, it doesn't stir up painful memories, does it?"

"No, only the good ones."

"So you really like that...um...lifestyle."

"Yes, I do. It surprises me too. I grew up as a modern, liberated woman, but suddenly, I found myself craving what Stephen gave me. Are you shocked?"

"Shocked? Hell no. You're like every man's wet dream." He blushed. "I mean that in a good way."

She laughed. "Trust me, I know. I like the anticipation as much as you do."

"That's it, isn't it? The anticipation before the event. The lack of underwear was just the first sign. This Stephen must've read you pretty well."

She took a bite of her sandwich to delay her answer. "It's strange, sitting here, talking to my new lover about my old lover."

"Yeah. It is, isn't it?"

"I mean most men wouldn't even want to think about any other men in my life. But you seem eager to hear all the details."

"Well, I admire him. And I envy him too."

"Why? Because he knew how to push my buttons?"

"Yes, that and he seemed so confident. In charge."

DeeDee nodded. She ate some more. Silence fell between them. "You worry that you can't be that confident?"

He shrugged. "I feel confident with women. Most women. But I'm always trying to tread lightly, not to say or do the wrong thing, you know. Some women are pretty touchy about equality and all."

"Well, sure. We only got the vote sixty years ago. We tend to be touchy."

"Then why do you like to be subservient?"

"If I had to use my amateur psychology, I'd say it was because I lost my father when I was young. He was a strong but caring person and I think I really missed having that in my life."

Carl's eyes reflected his empathy with the painful memory. "I'm sorry. I didn't mean to pry."

"No. We've gone too far to stop now. Don't you think?"

"That's what I wanted to talk about. I've never felt as masculine as I did last night. It was a rush." He laughed. "Like being a caveman again. Today, I'm thinking I dreamt it, that maybe you'll be angry or embarrassed. But you're saying, it's okay. You enjoyed it too."

"Yes." She waited.

He finished his sandwich slowly, not responding. But DeeDee could see his stature change. He sat more erect. His face glowed with confidence and strength. She couldn't help but grin.

Finally, he looked up. "Here's what I want to do. I want to explore your relationship with Stephen in more detail. I want to help you relive those experiences. I want you—and me too, for that matter—to have some of the best sex either of us have ever had."

She stared at him, wondering if that was what she really wanted or if she was being foolish, trying to relive her life with Stephen. Even as she thought it, she knew she wanted to try.

"Okay. But, just in case, let's have a safe word."

He looked confused for a moment. Then, "Oh, yes, I get it. A word that says, 'back off'."

She nodded.

"What's your favorite flower?"

"Tulips."

"Then that'll be the word. Tulips. Okay?"

She lowered her eyes to the table. "Yes, Master."

Chapter Six

DeeDee knelt on the rug, naked. Her eyes were downcast. They were at her apartment. It had been a week since their first date. They had come a long way since that awkward conversation at her kitchen table. Each time they had gotten together, Carl had exerted more control over her — with her acceptance, of course. He never pushed her farther than she was ready to go. She was in this position because that was the way her old Master had ordered her to be whenever she was in his presence.

"Naughty Girl." She looked up at Carl, a slight smile on her face. Though her old master had called her Naughty Slut, Carl preferred the gentler name. She still got them mixed up, in her mind and her speech. "Tell me about the first time you went to Master's home. When was this?"

"Early June. Right after school let out, my junior year. Neither of us had wanted it to end for the summer, like before. So on the last Friday of the school year, he gave me his address and told me to drive by every Saturday. When I —"

"Would Master approve of that pronoun, Naughty Girl?"

"Um, no, Master Carl. When Naughty Girl saw the signal, she was to come in through the back."

"Did he give the signal right away?"

"No, he made Naughty Girl wait. It was more than a week before she saw the red 'S' on the post. Naughty Slut had been checking every day, riding by on her bike, or driving her car. That day, Naughty Girl had been on a bike. She dropped the bike in the backyard and came in through the rear door. Master had left it unlocked."

She looked up at Carl, but he merely nodded for her to continue.

"Naughty Girl came in and didn't see Master. But she had her instructions. She had to remove all her clothes, then kneel on the rug in the living room and wait."

"Just as you are doing now."

"Yes, Master Carl. My knees had to be about a foot apart, my back straight, my arms crossed behind my back, my head down."

"There's those pronouns again: 'My,' 'I.' Did you make mistakes like this for Master?"

She nodded. "Many times. Master had to punish me — I mean, Naughty Slut."

"Looks like I'll have to punish you too. What did he do?"

"He had those rulers. He used to spank Naughty Girl with them."

"Where?"

"On her bottom and…" Tears began to well up in her eyes.

"Where else, my little slut?"

"On…on…Naughty Girl's little tits."

"Go get me the ruler."

Without a word, she rose and went to the desk. She returned and handed him a wooden ruler.

"How many times did he strike you, that first day?"

"I—Naughty Girl doesn't remember. Not many. He seemed happy to see his Naughty Girl. When I—Naughty Slut slipped a few times, he spanked me—her—on the bottom, then…a couple of times on the tits. It really hurt."

"You're really having trouble with your pronouns. I'm going to spank your bottom now. Put your head down and present yourself."

She obeyed, shaking slightly. The pale globes of her ass begged to be spanked. He had no desire to make the experience too painful for her, so he gave her just four swats on her ass, two on each cheek. The marks flared red against her skin.

"Th-thank you, Master Carl." Her voice was muffled by the rug.

"Now, for the tits."

She sat up. More tears flowed, but her face shone with barely concealed excitement. She clearly enjoyed their little game.

"I'm only doing this to help you remember your place and to help you remember your old Master. How many times did he spank your tits, that first day?"

"T-twice."

"Twice? That's all?"

"T-t-twice on each tit." Her voice caught. "It hurt Naughty Slut."

"Well, you're already doing better in remembering your pronouns, so maybe this will be the end of it. Put your hands behind you and thrust out your tits at me."

She did as she was told, closing her eyes against the expected blows. Her breasts were medium-sized, but perfectly formed. "Oh, no. Naughty Girl must watch her punishment," Carl said.

She opened her eyes and set her face. Her lower lip trembled. He took pity on her and gave her light, stinging slaps to each side of her tits. She grimaced but made no other sound.

"Th-thank you, Master Carl," she said when he was done.

"Did Master hit you harder than that?"

She nodded, clearly fearful that he might do the same.

"Well, I'm not going to hit you any more, unless you force me to, okay?"

"Naughty Girl will be good, she promises."

"Tell me what else he did to you that day."

She smiled coyly. "He used his Naughty Girl. Many times."

"Did you like it?"

"Oh, yes. He made her come until she couldn't come any more."

"Did he punish you again before you left?"

Her eyes fell to the floor. "Yes, Master Carl."

"What for?"

"Naughty Girl failed to shave her pussy properly. He found some stubble."

"Come, show me if you have stubble now."

She rose fluidly and came to him, standing close. Carl loved the smell of her—the scent of womanly sex mixed with a tinge of perfume. He examined the folds of her pussy carefully, but could see no stubble anywhere. She trembled. "You seem to be quite smooth, here, slut."

"Oh, yes, Master Carl. Master got tired of shaving his Naughty Girl or making her shave, so he sent her to a salon for a series of Brazilian waxes to remove all the hair."

"Isn't that where they pull the hair out by the roots?"

"Yes, Master."

"Did it hurt?"

"Yes, Master."

"How old were you when this happened?"

She looked up at the ceiling, remembering. "Um, twenty-two, I think."

"And you've stayed smooth ever since?"

"Yes. Although Naughty Girl has to go in for some treatments occasionally."

That surprised him. "This is even after Master died?"

"Yes, Master Carl."

"Why is that? He won't know if you do or don't."

"Naughty Girl would know," she said simply.

"I think you really loved your Master, didn't you?"

She nodded, a single tear tracking down her face.

"Why? I mean, he didn't treat you like most men would've."

"Naughty Girl's not sure if she can explain. He was a powerful man, an important man. And he turned all of his attention onto this lowly slut. Naughty Girl needed it. She knows he loved her just as much as she loved him."

"I'm not going to try to replace him, you understand. That would be impossible. But together, we can relive some of the best moments of your lives together, okay?"

She nodded. "Very well, Master."

"How many times did you visit him over that summer?"

"Oh, I—excuse me, Naughty Girl doesn't know. Just about every weekend."

Carl decided to let that minor slip go. "What were some of your favorite games you played?"

"Oh, gosh, Naughty Girl would have to think. Any game that ended with a huge orgasm was fun. And there were lots of those."

"Tell me about some of them."

"There was Find the Naughty Slut. I—she would hide and Master would try to find her before the timer in the kitchen went off. If he did, he would spank Naughty Girl with a ruler six times. If he didn't, he would make love to Naughty Girl, very gently until she came."

"Take me back. Share a game with me."

She looked wistful for a minute. Then she closed her eyes and began to speak.

"It was hot. July, probably. Naughty Girl saw the signal and came in, all tingly and horny. She stripped down and knelt on the rug. Master came in. He was naked too. He came close and stood right in front of her. Naughty Girl opened her eyes and saw his hard cock. She wanted to suck it. He let her for a few minutes then he said he wanted to play 'Find the Slut'. He explained the rules.

"He gave me five minutes to find a hiding spot. Master had a ranch-style house, so there weren't many places to hide. He closed his eyes and put headphones on while Naughty Girl hid. I hid in the closet in his bedroom the first time. He set the timer for ten minutes then came to look for his slut.

"He found her within five minutes. He dragged her out and took her to the living room. He had her kneel down with her bottom in the air and he gave six good whacks. Slut's bottom was very sore.

"Then he said, 'Let's play it again.' Naughty Girl didn't want to get another spanking, so she searched hard for a hiding spot. I finally hid behind the door of the laundry room. He missed me —"

"Girl, come here."

She stopped, and her face indicated she just realized she had used the wrong pronouns again.

"I'm sorry, Master Carl. I mean, Naughty Girl is sorry."

"Present your tits."

"No, please! Not the tits!" He could still see red marks on the sides.

"I'll give you a choice, Slut. You can take twelve swats on your behind, or four on your tits — two on each one. What'll it be?"

She blanched. Twelve was a lot, he knew. And four was just tolerable on her breasts, especially if they were light, like the last ones.

"T-t-tits, Master Carl."

"Present them."

She arched her back toward him. This time, she kept her eyes open.

He took the ruler and gave her a crack on the top of her right tit. She squealed — she couldn't help herself.

"That's good for two swats on your bottom as well," he said.

She made no sound as he struck her left one, although twin tracks of tears flowed down her cheeks. "Naughty Girl does not say 'I' or 'me' — Naughty Girl is simply Naughty Girl," Carl said as he snapped the ruler from underneath, catching the tender underside of her breast.

"Ow! Ow! Girl is sorry! She's sorry!"

"That's two more for your bottom."

She bit her lip and waited for the final blow to the underside of her left breast. It made a sharp noise in the room. She wiggled about, barely managing to keep quiet.

"And that's two more for wiggling. Present yourself."

She turned around quickly and raised her bottom for him. "Did Master have this much trouble with you?"

"Only at the beginning," she said, her voice muffled. "Naughty Slut learned quickly."

"Well, let's hope you do this time around, too." Carl gave her six sharp raps with the ruler, leaving nice red marks.

This made him extremely horny. "Okay, turn around and give your Master some pleasure. Don't swallow until I say."

DeeDee eagerly came to Carl and unzipped his pants. His cock sprung free. She took it into her mouth. She was truly an expert at cock-sucking. She licked and stroked him, her mouth active. In just minutes, she brought him off and he came heavily into her mouth. He pulled free and she opened her mouth to show the white sperm within.

He moved down until he could reach her pussy. "Swallow," he said, just as he pressed his fingers against her clit. She came immediately, conditioned as she had been by Master. The taste of sperm and an orgasm. Carl suspected by now, she might be able to come just from the act of swallowing sperm.

She clung to him, sobbing with both pain and release. The red marks on her breasts, he knew, would soon fade to blue, reminding her that she was no longer a person, but a slut. He wasn't sure how he felt about that. After all, he considered himself a decent sort of man—yet here he was, abusing this poor, sweet girl. She did love it, of course. *Just a while longer*, he told himself. *Let's see just how far she'll go.* He'd never felt like this before. He'd never met anyone like her.

"Remember," he whispered into a perfect, shell-shaped ear. "You are a Naughty Girl. You are here to give me pleasure, just as you gave your Master pleasure. Your needs are secondary."

She was nodding, remembering those same words from years past.

"Now, as I recall, you were telling me about a hide and seek game with Master. Please continue."

She sat up gingerly and tried not to let her bottom touch the rug. "Naughty Girl hid behind the door in the laundry room and although Master looked in, he didn't see his Slut. He left to look elsewhere. The timer went off before he could track his Girl down," she said, seeming to have no further problems remembering the correct pronouns.

"So he took his Girl to the bedroom and laid her on the clean sheets." Her voice became dreamy. "He ate his Naughty Girl's cunt for a long time. She had orgasm after orgasm. When she finally begged him to stop, he slipped his hard cock into her. She wrapped her legs about him and Slut came one last time with him."

"That was a good story. We'll have to play that game too. But right now, I have more questions."

"Yes, Master Carl."

"Usually, a slut is a woman who fucks many men. Did you remain exclusive to your Master?"

She looked down at the floor and he knew there was another tale to tell.

Chapter Seven

Naughty Girl began to cry again. This was clearly a painful memory to her. "Girl is sorry, Master. She never expected her old Master would want to share her."

"When did this happen?"

"It was about two years after Girl started seeing Master. The summer of my senior year. Hot day. Slut saw the signal and came in and she was shocked. There was a man, sitting with Master, on the couch. He was big, bald, middle-aged. He looked strong, mean. I—Naughty Slut hesitated. She wasn't sure what she was supposed to do.

"Master said to me, 'Why is my Naughty Slut just standing there?'"

"I said, 'I didn't know you had company.' His Slut even used the wrong pronoun, she was so shocked."

"Master told me he was an old college friend of his, just in for a visit. He said his name was Master Turk. He owned some sort of bondage club in San Francisco. Then he said, 'I told him all about my Naughty Slut. How obedient she was—looks like I was wrong.'"

"His Slut knew what she had to do then. But it was very hard. My Master just stared at his Slut until she took off all her clothes, right there in front of them. I was mortified."

"There's that pronoun again."

"Slut knows. She was making similar mistakes with Master. His friend confused me—his Slut—so much."

It also hurt her, Carl could tell. They'd had this private little thing going, and suddenly, Evers brought in a stranger and expected DeeDee to perform for him as well. He wasn't sure he was going to enjoy this story as much as the others. His conscience began to bother him again.

"So you were just twenty-two years old at this time, right?"

"Yes, Master."

"I can tell this story is different from the others. It brings up a lot of emotions. Would you rather not tell it?"

"It's all right, Master Carl. Naughty Girl knows you'd like to hear it."

"Yes I would. But I'll tell you what... Because this is such a personal story, I'll suspend the ban on personal pronouns. I want to know what you were really feeling during this time, okay?"

She looked up at him and smiled. "Thank you, Master Carl."

She gathered her thoughts and continued, "So after I was naked and assumed the position, I thought I was going to faint. I could hear them talking about me as if I was an object, like a shiny new car. 'Oh, she's a fine-looking whore,' Master Turk said. 'Look at that cute little butt on her. And those cupcake tits! Is she an obedient slut?'

"My Master said, 'Yes, but she has a lot to learn, I'm afraid.' He told him how we met and everything. I was blushing so much I was sure they could both tell from across the room.

"Then they got up from the couch and approached me. I thought Master would make me fuck this man and I didn't want to. He scared me. For one thing, he was bigger and meaner-looking than my master. Also, becoming intimate with Master had taken months, you remember. That I was suddenly supposed to just spread my legs for this stranger was something I didn't think I could do."

Carl wanted to hold her, to stroke her. But he wasn't sure if it would interrupt the flow of the story. He decided to wait.

"Then Master said, 'Naughty Slut, my friend would like to feel your soft mouth on his cock.' I nearly ran from the room, but my legs wouldn't work. Instead, I found myself obeying him, as I had been conditioned to all those years."

Her face got that glazed quality to it again. The images must have been stark in her mind.

"So I unzipped this man's pants and eased his cock out. He was bigger than Master. It was as if I was holding a snake. In a trance, I opened my mouth and put it around the head of that huge cock. There was no way that whole thing would fit in my throat, I knew. Still, I just did what I'd been trained to do. I started to suck him off as best I could."

"Did he come?"

"Yes, but it took a long time. I couldn't get him deep enough, so I used my hand on his shaft to stimulate him. He seemed to like it just fine, though. When he came, it was like I had put my mouth on a garden hose. Squirt after squirt flooded my mouth. I began to choke—there was no way to swallow it all. It spilled out around his cock and ran down my chin."

She paused there and Carl could tell she was remembering something important.

"It's funny, but despite my embarrassment and my anger at Master, the taste of that man's sperm suddenly caused me to come—and he hadn't even touched me! It wasn't a big orgasm, but I was surprised that it happened at all. I guess I'd really been trained by Master."

"What happened next?"

"Well, Master started to get angry because so much sperm had spilled out, but the stranger put his hand on Master's arm and said, 'Don't punish her on my account, Steve. She's a natural cocksucker.' "

"How did that make you feel?"

"Pleased—and grateful. Pleased that I had learned how to give pleasure so well, and grateful that this man would try to stop Master from punishing me. It wasn't something I expected from him."

"Did he succeed in that?"

"Not quite. I think Master wanted to show off a little. He seemed, well, different that day. More boastful or something."

Carl could understand that. Evers had an old college friend come by for a visit and he naturally wanted to show off. He had a rather dull career, and the most exciting thing in his life he couldn't share with anyone—that was, anyone except for an old friend that he trusted completely.

"Master said okay, he wouldn't punish me as much as he was going to, but he still needed to show his Slut the error of her ways. Then he said to his friend, 'I'll let you punish her. That way you can decide how much punishment she deserves.' He ordered me to get a ruler and assume the position. I still had sperm on my chin and tits—Master wouldn't let me wipe it off. I kneeled down with the side of my face against the rug. I could see Master Turk — this stranger — approach me.

"He took the ruler and Master said, 'I was prepared to give her ten or twelve spanks, but you decide what is fair.' When he hit me the first time, I almost fainted. He hit so hard!

"I was scared, but I shouldn't't've been. He gave me two more hard slaps on each cheek, then said I'd had enough."

Between her legs, juices were beginning to flow. They glistened on her upper thighs. This story, though somewhat painful, still aroused her.

"Did the stranger fuck you?"

"No. I feared he might. I thought Master had given him permission, but I was wrong." Her brows furrowed.

"What's wrong?"

"I just remembered something my master said — for some reason, I had forgotten it until now."

"Yes?"

"They were talking like I wasn't there, like I was part of the furniture. He said to Master Turk, 'I worry about her sometimes, if something should happen to me. She's so perfectly conditioned, I'm afraid she might fall into the hands of someone who doesn't understand how to use her.' And Master Turk said, 'Oh, leave that to me.' I remember it send chills through me, although I don't know what he meant."

Carl didn't either, but it seemed moot now. "I wouldn't worry about it. Evers has been dead for quite a while now. It was probably just idle talk."

She nodded. "I suppose so. He was probably just trying to embarrass me. I guess it was all just part of our game. We were making it up as we went along."

"Yes, we're doing much the same. I've never met a woman quite like you."

"I like it that you are not threatened by my memory of Master. He was a big part of my life, as you can tell."

"You know what's funny?"

"What?"

"I think I would have liked your Master. I understand him."

"Why do you say that?"

"Because I've been feeling those same feelings he did, back when you first sat on that chair in front of him in his office. He'd been looking for something—he didn't even know what—but when you walked in, he knew what he wanted."

"And you know what you want?"

"I didn't until I met you."

She smiled and looked at the ground. She murmured something softly.

"What's that?"

She looked up. "I don't know why I'm like this. I think of myself as a strong, independent woman, yet I crave this, being submissive. I fall right back into old habits when you get me talking about Master."

Carl nodded. "The words 'Naughty Slut' or 'Naughty Girl' seem to trigger that in you. When I use it, or order you to use it, you revert back to those old memories, triggering those tremendous orgasms again."

She just nodded, her face blank. He softened his tone. "Know that I'll protect you, DeeDee. I won't let this get out of control."

She looked up, searching his face. "Really? You promise? Because I've never been able to trust anyone like I did Master."

He cupped her chin in his fingers. "Trust is earned, DeeDee. I hope to earn it from you."

Chapter Eight

Carl lived in a small house about three miles from DeeDee's place. Because he wanted DeeDee to relive her experiences with Master, Carl decided to set up the same conditions. He told her to drive by the house every day, and only stop if she saw the red "S" on the porch. He'd found a big wooden letter at a hardware store and painted it himself.

For a week, he purposely didn't hang it out, knowing that she would become more anxious with each passing day. Finally, on Saturday, he put it up about ten a.m. Within an hour, he heard a noise at the back door.

DeeDee came in, her head down and appeared not to even notice him sitting on the couch. She wore a skirt and a yellow t-shirt—no underwear, of course. Flat sandals adorned her feet. She began to remove her clothes, piling them neatly on an upholstered chair. When she was completely naked, she dropped to her knees, spread them wide and bowed her head. Her hands went behind her back.

"Your Naughty Girl is here, Master Carl."

"Very good." Carl was very pleased to see her. His cock, more so. "Come here."

She scooted over quickly, staying on her hands and knees. Without being asked, she unzipped his pants and let his hardened tool spring free. DeeDee opened her mouth and took it in.

"How do you know that's what I want?"

She froze then pulled back. "I'm sorry, Master."

"Who's sorry?"

"N-naughty Girl," she stammered.

"Don't forget," I reminded her.

"Naughty Girl won't, she promises," she said.

"Very well, you may suck my cock now."

She returned to her duties. Carl closed his eyes and let the sensation wash through him. Her head moved smoothly up and down his shaft, as her right hand wrapped around the base and massaged him. Carl didn't want to come yet, so he stopped her after a few minutes. She looked disappointed.

"Later," he assured her. "But first, I brought you a present."

Her eyes grew wide. "For Naughty Girl?"

He pulled a box from under the couch cushion. She gasped and brought a hand to her mouth. He held it out to her and she took it tentatively. Her hand trembled as she opened it. Inside, she could see small gold rings connected by a fine chain. They looked like round little fishes.

She looked up, questioningly.

"They're nipple clamps."

Her mouth dropped open. He thought he detected fear in her eyes.

"No, no—they won't hurt you. At least, they're not supposed to. Here." Carl took one out and squeezed the tail of the fish together, showing her how it expanded the smooth band of gold. "These just grip the nipples—they don't pinch them."

"They're beautiful."

"Here, let me put them on you." She straightened up, thrusting her breasts out toward him. He could tell her nipples weren't extended enough, so he leaned down and suckled one gently. It grew in his mouth to full length. When he was satisfied, he pulled away and gently encircled it with the gold band, making sure it was seated low, then released the tension. It shrunk around her nipple, fitting perfectly. The chain hung straight down.

"It's beautiful," she said again.

Carl took the other clamp at the end of the chain and repeated the process to her left breast. Once they were in place, the chain hung between them in a graceful bow.

"Do they hurt?"

She shook her head. Tears began to flow from her eyes. "Naughty Girl l-l-loves them," she sobbed.

Her reaction surprised him. "I hope those are tears of joy," he joked.

"Master — how did you know?"

He was taken aback. "Know? Know what?"

Her eyes searched his face. "That Master Stephen gave his Naughty Slut jewelry for her body."

"Ohhh." He nodded. He sensed another chapter coming. "Tell me about it. What did he give you first?"

She touched the clamps, as if remembering. "Earrings," she said, nodding. "Little gold earrings that were shaped in a loose 'S' "

She didn't have to tell him what that stood for.

"You wore them all the time for him?"

"Yes."

"Did people ask what the 'S' stood for?"

"Sometimes. They were very stylish 'S's', so most people didn't recognize them as letters."

"When they did, what did you tell them?"

He could see tears in her eyes. "Master made me say."

"Say what, exactly?"

"That the 'S' stood for Slut."

He could imagine the embarrassment that caused her. Another step in her training. He could tell that the memory of it turned her on, despite her shame. A blush spread across her upper chest and the scent of her sex increased in the room. "What happened to them?"

Naughty Girl stared at the floor. For a moment, he thought she wasn't going to answer.

"Slut still has them, packed away."

The words came out before he fully thought about them. "I'd like to see them. Next time you come over."

She just nodded, her head hung low.

"Is this painful, my Naughty Girl?"

"No," she said at once, then softer, "Yes. A little."

"I won't spoil the memory of your old Master. But I'd still like to see them." A thought struck him. "Did he give you other items?"

Again the nod, eyes low. "Look at me," he said. When her head came up, Carl could see the tears had begun to track down her beautiful face. "Tell me."

"He, um, he gave his Slut...nipple rings," she said so softly he had to lean in to hear.

"Nipple *rings*?" Carl's eyes went to her nipples. DeeDee nodded in response to his question. "So you had your nipples pierced?" Another nod. He unfastened one of the clamps and spotted a small indentation on the side, partially grown back. He refastened the clamp. "What else?"

"My-my-my labia," she whispered. She forgot her pronouns again. Carl was too shocked to call her on it.

"Show me."

She stood and brought her groin close to his face. He bent down and saw the indentations here as well—two on each side. He felt strangely excited.

"Why did you stop wearing them?" Carl was pretty sure he already knew the answer.

"When he died, I—Naughty Slut couldn't bear the thought of wearing them again. They were just for him."

He nodded. "We will honor those wishes," he told her. "But I still want to see them, next time you come, all right?"

"Yes, Master Carl."

"Now, I want to see how my jewelry looks when we make love." Carl took off his pants then laid back against the sofa cushions. His cock stood up straight. He nodded to DeeDee and she straddled him immediately. Carefully, she reached between her legs to widen her slit with two fingers then lowered herself down onto his cock. She gave a little sigh.

Once she was fully seated, he reached up and tugged at the chain, tweaking her nipples. She closed her eyes and smiled, a small, shy, coy little smile. He liked the way the chain glinted in the light as she moved with him.

She was an energetic lover. When she was on top, she rocked and rolled, making sure his cock touched every part of her. Carl watched her face, her eyes closed, the beads of perspiration forming on her forehead. He could tell as she approached her orgasm. Her mouth began to hang open, her head dropped back, the sweat began to run down her body.

"Fuck!" She screamed, thrusting herself hard against his pubic bone, his cock wedged against her clit. She clung to him, shaking with release.

Chapter Nine

Carl had wanted to see her much more often, but work interfered. He had a particularly large project due, so much of his early evening hours were spent at the office in front of a computer.

Still, he never stopped thinking about her.

DeeDee was unique. *She's like the prototype perfect woman*, he thought. He knew women's libbers everywhere would be breaking out the hatchets if he dared speak it aloud, but he didn't care. To Carl, this just proved that there were women out there who enjoyed this kind of play. And Carl used the word play deliberately. He wasn't forcing DeeDee to act this way. She could've stopped him at any time with her safe word. She was as turned on by her memories of Evers as Carl was reliving them with her.

He made sure he protected her. He never took her too far and never violated her own inner limits. They were a very happy couple. Within a very short time, Carl was ready to have her move into his house and be his lover full-time, but she told him she wasn't ready. To Carl, that proved that she still retained power. If he were her true master, she would not have been able to refuse him. But Carl just told her to take her time, just being around her was enough for now.

Carl continued to exert more of his own power over her during their explorations of her relationship with her old master. He couldn't help himself. It not only felt right, but DeeDee was a willing participant. It had started right up the next time she came over to his house. She had kneeled on the rug before him, naked, as usual.

"Did you bring the jewelry?"

She nodded, then rose quietly and went to her purse. Fishing out a small box, she brought it over. Her eyes were wet.

"Here, Master Carl," she said softly, putting the box in his hand.

He took it carefully, as if it were the crown jewels. Opening it, he saw two gold nipple rings, what appeared to be a belly-button ring and four small gold rings that had to be for her labia.

"Show me where these went." He handed her the four rings.

She took the rings and held them carefully in the palm of her hand. Carl could see her lower lip trembling. Her memories must have been spilling over.

"Is it too painful? Would you rather not?" Carl felt he'd gone too far.

"Will Master Carl make Naughty Girl wear them?"

"No, not if it's too painful a memory."

Nodding, she came over and sat down next to him on the couch. She spread her legs and grabbed the fleshy lips. "Here," she said, showing him the tiny indentations, dots of white against the skin, two on each side. She held up one of the small gold rings, a shiny contrast to her pale smoothness.

"He had you pierced?"

"Yes. He took me to a friend of his, a woman who had a lot of piercings in her body. I was surprised he knew someone like that. After all, he'd been a professor for many years. He told me he had a secret life and now that he had met me, he could explore it more."

"What was that life?" He already knew the answer.

"He corresponded with members of a bondage and discipline club."

"Like that Master Turk?"

"Yes."

"Did you ever see him again?"

"No."

"Did Master Stephen ever force you to make love to anyone else?"

"No, he didn't. Thank god."

Carl decided to move on. "Did it hurt to be pierced like that?"

"A little. The woman numbed it up first."

"Why did he do that?" he asked.

"He-Master liked to tie his Naughty Girl's pussy up…and do…other things." Her voice was almost inaudible.

"What kinds of things?"

She hung her head. He couldn't imagine what her Master would make her do.

"H-he hung bells from them, for example."

"Bells?"

She nodded. "On little gold chains. They'd hang down an inch or so. They…they would tinkle when Slut moved."

Carl began to see how this could be quite embarrassing. "He'd take you out in public like that?"

"Not around here," she said. "We'd drive somewhere, where no one knew us. When we stopped, he'd ask me if I wanted to wear panties. It was our little game. I always said no, just like he expected me to, just like when we were in his office. Then he'd clip on the bells, telling me I was bad and had to be punished." She seemed to shake with the power of the memory. Carl could see her pussy was slick with juices. The effect on her was obvious.

He was so taken with the story that he had quite forgotten that she had stopped calling herself Naughty Girl. Carl's cock thrust hard against his pants. "Then what?"

"He'd make me get out of the car and walk with him. People could hear the bells, but didn't know where the sound was coming from. They'd turn and look. Once in a while, someone would look down and catch sight of the tiny bells, hanging right about the level of the hem of my short skirt and they'd laugh. I was mortified."

"But all you had to do was wear panties and he'd stop, right?"

"Yes." Carl had to lean in to hear her. "But I-I liked it. I couldn't help myself."

"Why is that, do you think?"

"I-I don't know. I think I liked being a naughty girl. At least, with him."

"So you both enjoyed public displays like this?"

DeeDee just nodded.

"It turned you on." Carl could hardly believe his ears.

Again, the nod.

"Bring me your clothes," he ordered, an idea forming in his head. He wondered if he had the nerve.

She looked up sharply at him, her eyes questioning, but she said nothing. She rose fluidly, a sheen of wetness on both thighs and went to her pile of clothes. She'd worn a black skirt that came down to just above her knees and an ivory silk blouse with tiny pearl buttons. A pair of black sandals completed her outfit.

"I suppose this will have to do."

"W-what do you mean, Master Carl?"

"This skirt is too long, but it's all you've got. I think the blouse is all right, if we unbuttoned a couple of buttons. The shoes could be a little higher too."

She looked confused, glancing down at her nakedness then up to his face. "You want me to put on my clothes?"

"Yes. We're going shopping."

She dressed quickly, clearly nervous. She started to head to the bathroom then stopped to ask permission. "I'm-I'm wet. Down there. May I go wipe up, Master Carl?"

"No. And you'll have to be spanked for using that euphemism. What word should you have used?"

"P-pussy." The word came out softly.

"Or?" he pressed.

"Cunt."

"Get the ruler."

She rose and went to his desk, then returned with a wooden ruler. Carl could see red marks high on her cheekbones. She appeared flushed and nervous.

"Get into position." She dropped down and turned around in front of him, presenting her ass. He flipped up her skirt and gave her two quick whacks on each rounded globe, leaving red stripes. He did not hit her too hard. Just a wake-up call.

He escorted her to the car and they drove to the mall. On the way, he made her raise her skirt up so he could see her nakedness. She seemed flushed and yet strangely excited. When they arrived, he turned to her. "You've also forgotten your pronouns, you know. You'll have to be punished for that."

She blanched. Carl could tell she thought he was going to spank her here. "No, not that," he added, seeing a visible sign of relief in her eyes. "I want you to roll up your skirt a little bit."

DeeDee opened her mouth to say something then quickly closed it. She attempted to obey him while still sitting down, but he stopped her with a hand on her forearm. "No, get out of the car first."

Her eyes widened. "You want me...um, Naughty Girl to get out and raise up her skirt?"

"Are you being disobedient? Does Naughty Girl need more punishment?"

"No, no, sir." She got out, leaving the door open as a shield. Carl watched her from inside the car. Nervously, she rolled up the skirt an inch.

"Keep going," he said.

Another inch disappeared. Now it came to mid-thigh. "A little more."

She made an inarticulate sound and looked around fearfully. She rolled the skirt until he could see the slick juices on both of her inner thighs. The skirt hung just about two inches below her damp pussy. "Okay, that'll do."

He got out and locked the car. She came to him, nervous as a cat. He leaned over and unbuttoned the top two buttons of her blouse. She looked very slutty. She also seemed to vibrate in her shoes.

"Is this what Master would do?"

She nodded, her eyes wide. She looked around, as if she was prepared to hide if someone saw her. But that was the whole point, wasn't it?

Carl started to walk. DeeDee raced to catch up. "Oh, and one more thing. While we're inside, don't forget your name."

He thought DeeDee would faint. He could see her blushing all the way up the front of her chest to the tips of her ears.

They entered the mall and strolled over to a young women's store, someplace that would cater more to girls from teenage to college years, not a twenty-seven year-old like DeeDee. Rock tunes played loudly and colored lights spiraled around, making the store look like a rave.

Carl went up to a Goth clerk, hair dyed black with a purple stripe, a silver ring piercing an eyebrow and a nose ring through one nostril. Perfect, he thought. "My girlfriend needs some new clothes," he said over the boom of the music.

She stared at DeeDee, her eyes moving up and down, taking in the altered outfit, the loosened buttons. "Yeah," she said, her mind clearly working as she glanced back at Carl. "I think I can fix her up. And I'll bet you'll want to approve everything."

He nodded. The girl was quick.

She grinned and took DeeDee by her elbow and steered her toward a display in the back. As Carl followed, he heard her say, "I'm Sammy, what's your name?"

He almost laughed out loud as he saw DeeDee's shoulders shudder, then she leaned in to tell the girl, "N-naughty G-Girl."

Sammy turned almost completely around to stare at Carl. He just smiled and tried to appear innocent.

Sammy took her to a rack of short skirts of various types: Denim, leather, a soft stretchy Lycra, all in many colors. Together, Sammy and Carl picked out some he liked. Naturally, he approved of a red Lycra miniskirt first. A black leather one came next, then a shiny blue micro-miniskirt. They brought the outfits to the dressing room, which was a narrow aisle with cubicles on either side. A full-length three-sided mirror stood at the far end.

"There's no one in there right now if you want to go in with her," Sammy told him.

"No, that's all right. I'll stand out here. You help her, okay?"

She went in with a visibly nervous DeeDee. He could see that the sheen on her legs had increased. The swinging door shut and he could hear them over the music in the background, talking about the skirts, then suddenly, there was silence.

Carl couldn't help but lean in to listen. He heard Sammy say softly, "You're not wearing any panties!" A moment later, "And you're all wet. Do you want a tissue?"

There was silence. Carl could only assume DeeDee was shaking her head.

"Does your boyfriend make you do this?"

For a minute, he thought DeeDee wouldn't answer. Then: "Yesss."

"Why do you let him?"

There came another pause, then, softly: "Naughty Girl likes it."

"Wow, you're a weird one, lady, if you don't mind me saying."

The door opened and Sammy came out, followed by DeeDee in a ridiculously short red skirt that clung to every curve. She still wore her ivory blouse, which now looked mismatched somehow. The color was right, but the style...

"Wow," Carl said. "You look great. But that blouse doesn't work." He turned to Sammy. "Can you find something that would go with this?"

She nodded, telling him she had just the thing. She disappeared. Carl stared at DeeDee's crotch and made her turn around. Her face remained pink, making a nice contrast with the red skirt.

Sammy came back with a couple of tops. They started to go back into the dressing cubicle but Carl stopped them. "No, she can put it on right here."

DeeDee's eyes got wider, if possible, and she glanced nervously around the nearly empty store. Nobody appeared to be paying any attention. "R-right here?"

Carl gave her a flat look. "'Right here', what?" he asked.

Her embarrassment grew. "R-right h-here, M-master Carl," she managed.

"Cool!" Sammy said brightly. They watched as DeeDee quickly unbuttoned and shrugged off her blouse. Her breasts jiggled as she hurried to put on the pink blouse offered by Sammy. It had three buttons at the top, and the material was meant to be tied underneath the breasts. DeeDee shrugged it on and buttoned it. When she tied it, she looked like a slutty Daisy Mae.

"Perfect," Carl said. "Now let's look at the leather skirt."

Both Sammy and DeeDee stared at Carl, questioning whether he wanted her to change that right out in the open as well. "Let's go over by the mirror and try it on, okay?"

DeeDee actually looked relieved to be farther into the dressing room — that is, until she came face to face with her reflection in the three-sided mirror. If anything, she felt more exposed now. She stared at her outfit, turning this way and that, and tugging at the edges of the skirt, trying in vain to cover her obviously aroused state.

Sammy brought out the leather skirt and they waited while DeeDee got up her nerve to disrobe. Carl turned to Sammy. "Do you have a ruler, by any chance?"

"A ruler?" Sammy had a puzzled look on her face.

That galvanized DeeDee into action. She stripped off the red skirt and pulled up the black leather one. She wasn't fast enough to avoid giving them all a show. Carl could see her labia were red and swollen, her slit dripping wet.

"Well, it looks like it's not needed now."

Sammy nodded in understanding and grinned at the mortified DeeDee. "I think that outfit calls for a different blouse, don't you, sir?"

Carl agreed. Just as Sammy brought out a yellow crop-top to try on, two teenagers rounded the corner and stopped, staring at the spectacle in front of them, their clothes forgotten in their hands.

"Don't mind us, ladies," Carl said at once. "You might even be able to help us decide. Do you think this blouse goes with this skirt?"

They approached warily. Sammy held up the new blouse over the pink one. "I don't think you can really tell that way. Go ahead and put it on," he told DeeDee.

Flaming red now, she unbuttoned the blouse and handed it to Sammy. Taking the other one, she put it on so quickly Carl thought she'd sprain a shoulder.

The teens gaped at the sight of her naked breasts then giggled to each other.

"Or do you think this skirt goes better?" he held up the micro-mini. He could see DeeDee's eyes pleading with him.

"Gee, I dunno. I'd have to see it on her," one of the pimply faced girls said.

Carl laughed inwardly. *Girls can be so cruel!*

"Yes, let's see it."

DeeDee turned away from them in an effort to gain a small measure of privacy, only to see herself in 3-D once again. Sammy handed her the skirt. For a brief moment she hesitated. Carl took one of the empty wooden hangers and held it sideways, as if he was preparing to spank her. DeeDee stripped off the leather skirt and quickly stepped into the micro-skirt. Carl waggled his finger, making her turn around.

"What do you think, ladies?" he said, pretending they were sophisticated shoppers.

"Oooh, it looks cool," said one.

"Yeah," giggled the other, pointing to between DeeDee's legs, "but it looks like she could use a little clean up on aisle two!"

They dissolved into laughter. Her friend pulled her away before any more could be said. Carl imagined the girls thought they were all nuts. When they were gone, he turned to Sammy again. "We'll take it all. Oh, and do you mind if Naughty Girl gets fingerprints on the mirror?"

Sammy looked puzzled all over again. "Um, no, but what—"

"Naughty Girl, lean over and put your palms flat on the glass."

Carl thought DeeDee might melt into the floor. He realized he might be going too far, but he couldn't resist the feeling of power it gave him. She remained perched on that delicious teeter-totter between stimulation and orgasm, embarrassment and release. Carl kept a close eye on her and tried to push her only as far as her old Master would've.

DeeDee leaned against the mirror, bending over at the waist. Her micro-skirt rode up, exposing half of her ass. He took the wooden hanger and—

"Okay, that's enough," Sammy said. "This is just too weird. I want you guys to leave before my boss gets here."

Carl had expected that. He wasn't really sure if he was prepared to spank DeeDee right in the store. He knew if he did, she'd probably come in a knee-buckling orgasm.

Now she'd have to wait a little longer.

"Very well," he said, trying to look disappointed. "She'll wear what she's got on out of the store."

Sammy rang up the purchase. All the while, the other patrons were staring at them. Apparently, the two teens had spread the word. DeeDee just stood there, legs clasped tightly together, trying to pull down her tiny skirt, while her nipples poked tents in her yellow shirt.

When they left, DeeDee turned immediately toward the parking lot.

"Wait," Carl said. She froze.

"We need to get you some new shoes."

"Shoes?! Please, Master," she whispered. "I can't get shoes dressed like this. They'll see me!"

"Pronouns," he warned. "Try again."

"P-please, Master. Naughty Girl can't get shoes dressed like t-this. They'll see m-my p-pussy."

Carl nodded. "That's better. Didn't your Master ever take you shopping?"

DeeDee bit her lip. Finally, she nodded.

"Did he take you to try on shoes, dressed in a short skirt?"

"N-n-not this short."

"Well, if you like, we can put on the leather one, that's longer." He started to reach into the bag.

She panicked, no doubt thinking he'd make her change right here in the mall. "No, no, Master Carl. This is fine. Just fine."

She walked in front of him as they headed to the shoe store. When they entered, Carl scanned the place, trying to find the right salesman for DeeDee. He spotted the perfect foil — a young, skinny redhead who probably hadn't gotten laid since, well, forever. He dodged around a smooth, oily salesman type — just the man who'd love to stare up DeeDee's skirt, and corralled the young man.

"Yes, can you help us?"

His eyes looked like silver dollars. His freckles seemed to glow. "Yessir, sir. Whatdja need?" His voice came in a rush. He cleared his throat. Behind Carl, he could hear the oily salesman curse under his breath.

"My girlfriend needs some high heels."

His head nodded up and down so fast Carl thought it might come off. "Over here, sir, um, ma'am. There's a nice selection. W-would this be for a f-f-formal occasion?"

"No, just for general wear," he said. The fact that Carl answered for DeeDee wasn't lost on the salesman. For her part, she just stood there like a statue, her legs tightly together.

Carl selected three pairs to try on, two black and one tan, but all had at least three-inch heels.

Wisely, the boy led them to a chair in the far corner of the store, and had her sit, facing sideways to the front. Still, everyone could see her long, beautiful legs stretched out in front of her.

"My name's Danny," he said by way of introduction.

"I'm Carl." He waited, looking at DeeDee.

Finally, DeeDee spoke for the first time. "N-naughty Girl," she whispered.

"Nau—" Danny was sure he had heard it wrong. "Naut—what?"

DeeDee was forced to say it again, louder. "Naughty Girl."

He rocked back on his heels, his mouth open. He looked around to see if anyone else heard. Oily salesman certainly had; he was biting his knuckle hard, looking pained.

Danny tried to get back on track. "Ooo-kay. Now, what size do you wear?"

"Why don't you measure, to make sure," Carl put in.

The boy tried to keep the grin off his face with little success. He retrieved the silver scale and slid it under one of DeeDee's delicate feet. She still had her legs tightly together. "Looks like a six," he said, trying to keep his eyes from wandering up her leg.

He disappeared into the back room. Oily salesman took the opportunity to drift by. "Everything all right here?" he inquired, hoping Carl might ask him to take over the sale.

"We're being helped," he said pointedly. "He's getting some shoes."

"Ah. Very well then." He looked disappointed. He finally drifted away. When Danny returned, Carl could see a bulge in his pants—not that he generally tended to observe such things.

The first pair of black pumps had four-inch heels. Better. Danny slipped them on. Carl noticed that DeeDee had allowed her legs to part just a little bit. It didn't take much to allow her nakedness to peek out from under her skirt. Danny pretended not to notice.

"How's that?"

DeeDee stood with some difficulty, trying to keep her legs together. She walked—no, tottered—around the room. She glared at Carl as if to ask him if he'd lost his mind.

"Are they comfortable?"

"Yes, but a little, um, tall," she said.

"You look good. Walk to the front and back."

Carl could see the redness flash on her cheeks like signal flags, but she obeyed without a word. Everyone in the store stared, as well as a few passing by outside, as DeeDee strolled carefully down the aisle then returned, careful to stay atop the teetering heels.

"Good. Those will do. Let's try on the tan ones now."

Danny eagerly stepped in as DeeDee sat. Her skirt rode up. She tried to pull it down, but caught Carl's eye. He shook his head. So she sat, her shoulders slumped, as Danny tried to concentrate on her shoes, the edge of her naked pussy showing out from underneath her skirt.

Carl sensed Oily Salesman returning. He hovered just out of earshot, probably straining his eyeballs as he took in the scene. Carl decided not to shoo him away, as it only increased DeeDee's lust and mortification. He felt as if he were someone else, perhaps the personification of Evers, back from the grave.

Carl decided to step back from the brink. He felt she'd had enough, so he rejected the tan shoes as soon as she stood up. He bought the black ones, which he made her wear out of the store.

DeeDee seemed grateful when he turned toward the lot. "Are you taking Naughty Girl home?" she whispered, her voice pleading.

"Yes, dear. I think you've had enough excitement for one day." He also wanted to take advantage of her passion. She had been on the verge of an orgasm for a couple of hours. He could only imagine what this might do to their lovemaking later.

Chapter Ten

"My god! Naughty Girl thought she was going to die of embarrassment!" DeeDee said as she slipped into the car. "Why did you make her do that?!"

"I don't really know," he answered truthfully. "At first, I thought we were just reliving some of your past adventures with Master Stephen, but it did seem to take on a life of its own, didn't it?"

"Yes, Master. Naughty Girl nearly came a couple of times!"

"Good. I imagine you were rather embarrassed."

"Embarrassed! I was mortified! But it was a controlled mortification, if that makes any sense."

Carl didn't call her on the pronoun. It seemed as if they had just exited a stage and now they could relax and get out of character.

"You mean, you knew I wouldn't go too far?"

"Something like that. I actually felt safe with you there. I never could've done that with anyone else, I don't think."

"Except Master Stephen."

"Well, yes."

"I'm glad it turned you on. It means you're all primed to make love to me."

She smiled. "You'd better. Or I'll have to call Frank."

Carl drove home in record time. By the time he parked, his erection was insistent. DeeDee beat him to the front door, and he could see at once that the back of her skirt was soaked with juices.

He grabbed her around the waist and hugged her close. "You know, if you just wore panties, you wouldn't have this leakage problem," he said, grinning.

"Fuck me, Master," was all she said.

Inside, they immediately began stripping off their clothes. DeeDee didn't have far to go—in seconds, she stood naked, watching Carl dancing around on one foot, trying to remove his pants. She giggled at the sight of him—his raging hard-on pressing against his boxer shorts. She waited patiently until he was naked too then ran ahead of him into the bedroom.

He chased her and caught up with her at the bed. He fell onto her, careful not to crush her and heard her squeal with delight. He held her face down while she gave a few mock struggles. He pressed his cock against her upper thigh. She quit squirming immediately and spread her legs for him.

Carl wanted her so badly, he couldn't bear to wait, and yet, he also wanted to prolong the moment—a moment they had been building to for a few hours now. He held her there, moving his cock in tiny circles, feeling the slickness on her leg. She waited there expectantly, thrusting herself back against him when he didn't immediately plunge into her.

"I love what you do to me," Carl whispered, allowing the tip of his cock to touch her hot core. He reached down and spread her labia apart. She gasped as he touched her. She was hot as if burning with fever.

"Fuck me, please," she begged, then added, "Master."

He held off a few more seconds, thinking his cock might explode in the meantime. Finally, he pushed his hard member into her, hearing her gasp. At the same time, he pressed down with three fingers on her clit. DeeDee came at once, vibrating against him, a moan escaping her lips.

Carl began to thrust in earnest now, knowing he couldn't hold back long. He loved the way his cock felt inside her, the slickness, the heat, the scent of her. He grabbed her hips and thrust hard, pumping in and out for a few critical seconds before he gasped and felt his release.

DeeDee pushed back against him and Carl knew she was having another orgasm. Sweat poured off their bodies. All of the events of the day culminated in this one base act—an act of love, obedience, trust and perversity. Especially perversity.

Carl never felt so good being bad. So why did it gnaw at him?

Later, when they were both completely satiated and had gotten up again, Carl felt a bit awkward around DeeDee. It surprised him. They'd done nearly every wicked thing two people could do and it had felt great—for a time. Now was he actually feeling some remorse? He wondered if she felt it too.

He was in the kitchen, having showered and dressed, fixing both of them a sandwich. He mulled over his conflicting emotions while DeeDee showered.

He had to admit to himself that he'd been taking advantage of her. Reliving her experiences with her old Master, enjoying the thrill of total control—it brought out the dark side of him. *Perhaps it's in all of us*, he mused.

But now he'd begun to feel guilty. He never expected to find someone like her, someone who would do anything to please him, no matter how embarrassing it might be. Sure, he knew she got off on it. *That's just part of who DeeDee is*, he told himself.

However, it's who she was with Evers, not me, he thought. *And I'm not Evers.*

That was it. That's why his conscience bothered him. He wasn't being honest; he was just using her. *That's not me. I'm a nice guy. Aren't I?*

Carl wasn't sure he even knew the real DeeDee. The one he'd rescued, the smart, pretty girl. She'd gotten lost somehow after he had discovered DeeDee the Slut.

Right then, he decided to back off the reminiscing for a while. When DeeDee came out of the shower, naked except for a towel wrapped around her head, Carl told her he didn't want her to use that "Naughty Girl" name for a while.

"Really?" she said, her eyes wide. She seemed confused.

"I know Evers called you Naughty Slut. And while I've thoroughly enjoyed revisiting that time, I feel like I'm trying to be somebody I'm not."

She gazed at him and for a moment, he thought she might cover up her nakedness, like Eve in the Garden of Eden. Innocence lost. Then she nodded, ever so slightly.

"I think you are a smart, beautiful, attentive and caring woman. A woman I'm lucky to have gotten to know," he continued. "At the same time, I think your experiences with Evers changed your perception of what a man should be in your life. We're not supposed to be your masters! I mean it's nice and all…" Carl trailed off, feeling foolish. How could he tell her that she was too easily exploited? That it might be dangerous in the wrong hands?

"Look, I just want to get to know the 'other' DeeDee. You know, the girl who reads poetry and literature, who dimples when she smiles, who trusted me when she hardly knew me—in other words, the woman I had expected to meet on our first real date together. Before I let my curiosity about your lack of underwear lead me into this fascinating and lurid tale about your submissive life with Stephen."

DeeDee stared at him for a long minute then reached out and placed a soft hand on his cheek. He immediately covered it with his hand then drew it toward his mouth and kissed it.

"I think," she started then stopped. "I think that would be…nice."

Carl felt he had disappointed her somehow. He wondered, not for the first time, if there was another woman behind the submissive slave she'd been for so many years. Maybe she didn't know how to relate to men otherwise? It would certainly explain how she could get mixed up with a creep like Frank.

"This doesn't mean we can't have some fun," he said lamely. "I mean, we can still play some games, you know, later on."

She took his hand to her lips and kissed it. "You're not trying to break up with me, are you?"

"No! Not at all!" He hoped she didn't think he was losing interest in her. "It's just that I want to separate me from your memories of Evers, that's all."

She leaned in and kissed him gently on the lips. "I think I'll go get dressed then," she said, and was gone.

Chapter Eleven

DeeDee spent the night with him. He awoke with her nibbling at his morning hard-on, teasing him, enticing him.

"Oh, honey," he said, pulling her back up to him, kissing her gently. "Let me wake up, huh? I should also take a leak and brush my teeth."

She nodded. "Sorry, Ma—I mean, Carl. My master used to like me to wake him with my mouth every morning when I stayed over."

Carl sat up. *Okay, that was just a little too creepy. It was time to get old man Evers out of my bed once and for all.*

"That's nice, DeeDee," he said, emphasizing her name. "But I'm not your old master. You don't have to do that for me."

She seemed to shake herself slightly. "You're right. I'm sorry. It's just that you remind me of him. Well, younger, of course. When I woke up, I kinda slipped back into my old ways."

"Perfectly understandable," he said. "And you don't have to apologize. But now I want you to get to know Carl Harman, the designer of cartoon characters and a struggling writer. Of course your story fascinated me. I thoroughly enjoyed it. Now I just want to put down the book for awhile and hang out with my girlfriend. Do you understand?"

A sly smile crept to her lips. "Yes. As long as you continue to fuck me like you did yesterday. I thought I'd explode. You may have short-circuited my wires somewhere."

He hugged her. "Oh, that'll be the day. But no worries — if you ever find the sex gets dull, you can just go back to calling me Master."

She touched his face. "Coffee?"

"You bet. I'm going to jump in the shower."

When he came out, his hair still damp, wearing boxer shorts, Carl found DeeDee, dressed in his robe, cooking up French toast. He came up behind her and pulled her to him by her hips. She giggled and rubbed her ass against him.

"Careful, you'll make me burn breakfast." She turned and gave him a peck on the cheek. He kissed her back, then untied her sash and reached in. She was naked underneath. He slipped his hands around her waist and pulled her tight. He let one hand slip down to her slit, where it came away wet and smelling of sex.

She pushed him away. "Whoa, big boy. You'll get all you want later. Right now, there's coffee ready and toast to flip." He let her go and she turned around, not bothering to close the robe. Carl poured himself a cup and sat down.

"So tell me," he asked. "How is it that a macho guy like Frank never uncovered your deep dark secret?"

She turned briefly to give him a baleful eye. "Frank? You seem worried about Frank a lot."

"Do I? Well, let's just call it writer's curiosity."

She shrugged. "He never asked."

"Would you have told him if he had?"

"I think so. Master had conditioned me to tell the truth. But Frank was far too wrapped up in himself to ask about my past. And I'm glad he didn't."

"Me, too." Carl shuddered to think what Frank would have done with DeeDee's amazing submissive side. Then again, he had experienced some of it, hadn't he? Otherwise, why would she have stuck with him all those months?

That was why DeeDee had been looking around that night at the bar, he suddenly realized. She was looking for someone like Stephen to replace Frank, who was a pale imitation of what she needed in a man. And Carl had obliged her.

They ate and drank coffee, and talked about inconsequential things. It was easy to be with her. Carl hated to have it come to an end, but he had a project looming. He looked at his watch. It was nearly ten.

"DeeDee, I've got to go. I'm sorry, but I've got this project that my client wants by the end of the week and if I don't get on it, I'll lose the business."

She nodded. "That's okay. I should be getting back home anyway, check on the fish."

A smile tugged at the edges of his mouth. "You don't have any fish."

She giggled. "Well then, I'd better pick some up on the way home." She rose. Carl stood too and gathered her into his arms before she could slip away. His cock sprang to attention.

"Maybe I have time for a quickie…" he suggested.

She grabbed his shoulders. "A quickie? You think I'll be satisfied with a mere quickie?"

"Um, probably not. So I guess I'll just have to wait until later, then…"

She gave him an elaborate sigh. "Oh, all right. A quickie is better than nothing, I suppose." She let her robe slip off her shoulders.

Carl was really beginning to fall in love with this girl, he decided.

Chapter Twelve

Carl intended to call DeeDee that afternoon, but his client dropped by his small office after five and stayed for nearly two hours, going over the designs, suggesting changes and editing copy. Carl didn't mind because he genuinely liked the work he had done, but like all clients, he wanted to put his stamp on it.

By the time he got home, it was half-past seven and he was exhausted. Carl checked his voicemail and email and was surprised not to have heard from DeeDee. He called while he heated up a microwave dinner, fully intending to beg off seeing her tonight. He just wanted to eat and go to bed. Even his cock didn't argue the point.

Oddly enough, she wasn't home. He got her voice mail and left a brief message, telling her he'd call her in the morning.

After a restful night, Carl woke up at eight-thirty, fully refreshed. He put on a pot of coffee and mentally organized his day. He had several corrections to do for his client, but they weren't overwhelming. He figured he could probably finish by early afternoon. Then the client would have to approve the final changes before Carl could put the document together for the printer by Friday. Idly, he wondered if DeeDee would like to have a dinner down by the waterfront.

He called her again. Once more, he got her answering machine. He actually began to get a little jealous, ridiculous as that sounded. He imagined that she had gone out last night with another man and was now sleeping next to him—maybe it was Frank! Carl reined in his childish reaction and left a simple, non-judgmental voicemail, then headed off to work, trying not to dwell on it. He told himself she probably had gone to bed early to rest up from all the lovemaking.

Carl concentrated on the project, doing some of the best work he felt he had done in months. Perhaps it was because getting laid helped clear up his mind. With the client's suggestions, he was better able to anticipate what he expected and Carl felt he had delivered on that promise. By three-thirty, he had gone as far as he could without more input from him, so he emailed the final draft to him, then shut down the computer and headed home.

On the way, he used his cell phone to call DeeDee one more time. Again, he got her voicemail. This was not like her. It was as if she had dropped off the face of the earth. Making a sudden decision, Carl turned the car toward her apartment.

Nervously, he knocked at No. 136, wondering what could have happened to her so suddenly. Dark thoughts invaded. He worried that she might be inside, unconscious on the floor. Or worse. Had Frank shown up suddenly, seeking revenge? The thought sent fingers of fear through him.

He knocked again before using the key she had given him to enter. The apartment looked clean and neat—no signs of a struggle. He moved into her bedroom and found everything in order. Her clothes were hanging in her closet, shoes neatly arranged on the floor. On her bedside, a book she had been reading remained, one page dog-eared to mark her place.

She didn't appear to have left town suddenly. Carl was beginning to feel foolish. No doubt she had simply stepped out for her own personal reasons and he was acting like a jealous idiot. Now he feared she might come home and catch him spying on her, so he wanted to leave quickly.

Before he did, he stopped in her bathroom. He couldn't say why, he just felt a need to check to see if her toothbrush was still there. What he saw froze him in place. In one corner of the mirror, written in lipstick, was: "Turk." The "K" was smeared, as if she had written it in a hurry.

A cold chill went through Carl. *Could it be*, he asked himself. It seemed impossible, yet he couldn't otherwise explain her sudden disappearance. Somehow, Master Turk had shown up and had "collected" her, perhaps using her ties to her old master to bind her to him or perhaps simply kidnapping her outright. Could that have happened? Or was his imagination working overtime? Then again, why else would she write that?

Carl went through the apartment again, this time looking for the smallest items a woman would want to take with her on a trip. He imagined himself to be her, standing naked in front of the glowering Master Turk, who is demanding that she pack a few things and go with him. Carl found her toothbrush and her makeup kit were missing, as were the new pair of black pumps with four-inch heels. He couldn't identify the dress she took, but he could picture that it would be simple—and short. Looking through her desk, he couldn't find a checkbook, so she probably had that with her as well.

However, Carl did find an old brokerage statement. DeeDee, his sweet little submissive princess, owned

$234,000 worth of stocks and bonds—no doubt courtesy of Master Stephen. No wonder she didn't have to work. And now she was in the clutches of this Master Turk, who was doing god knows what with her.

Carl's body went cold as he contemplated it. From the little he had heard her talk of him, he worried just what he might be up against. Master Turk didn't seem the type to be easily defeated, like Frank had been. And especially now, since Carl had no doubt that Turk had taken DeeDee back up to San Francisco, where he'd be secure, comfortable. Getting DeeDee away from him wouldn't be easy.

Then, on the other hand, Carl doubted he knew about him. He smiled slightly, thinking Turk was in for one hell of a surprise.

Carl called his client and explained that he had a "family emergency" that required him to be out of town for a couple of days. The client was sympathetic, though Carl knew he'd wanted this project to be completed by the end of the week.

He assured him he'd be back no later than Thursday and would work all night if he had to. Carl asked that he make all the final corrections and email them back. "I'll have it to the printer by Friday afternoon," he promised.

Little did he know that he wouldn't be able to keep that promise.

Chapter Thirteen

The drive from Santa Barbara to San Francisco took about six hours, including the slow-downs for traffic in the busy corridor along Highway 101 in the Bay Area. After packing a few items of clothing, Carl had left his house by five and had pulled into downtown San Francisco by 11:15 p.m. He hoped he wasn't on a wild goose chase.

On the way, he mentally tried to recall everything DeeDee had told him about Turk. Carl knew he ran a club in the city, something to do with bondage and discipline. Apparently, he was heavy into the BDSM scene. Had DeeDee mentioned the name of the club? Carl couldn't remember. So he had to wing it. He drove into the Tenderloin district, where all the seedy bars could be found and parked in a lot, paying an outrageous fee for them to watch his car for the next two hours.

Carl walked up the block, passing rundown bars, drunks trying to be his friend and hookers asking him for dates until he found a club that featured bondage acts, The Den of Iniquity. It seemed as good a place as any to start. He paid the fifteen-dollar cover charge and went inside. The Den was dark and loud, with just a few spotlights illuminating key areas. The rest of the club seemed bathed in a dim red light. A band shouted — not played — music from a small stage in one corner, but nobody paid them any attention. The action took place under the spotlights, where couples acted out bondage scenes.

Carl had heard of places like this, but never experienced them. Seeing people act like this in public made him a little ashamed of the way he had treated DeeDee. *It was just an experiment*, he told himself. *We were exploring our dark sides.* It didn't make him feel any better.

On one small, round stage, a woman was bent over a padded sawhorse, her hands and feet tied down, a gag in her mouth. A thin black leather thong framed her nearly naked ass and the only other clothing she wore was a black leather bra, a size too small. Her breasts lunged out the top.

Her "master" stood behind her with a whip of some sort. Perhaps it would be called a cat o'nine tails. He reared back and struck her, but the whip didn't seem to really hurt her — there were only faint marks on the round globes of her ass. Nevertheless, she screamed into her gag as if she was dying and the gawkers nodded appreciatively.

At another stage, a woman was being "tortured" with feathers. She, too, wore only a bra and a thong, and her mistress, by running the feathers over her exposed flesh, seemingly brought her to the brink of an orgasm again and again, stopping just in time. The girl writhed in comic agony. The crowd loved it.

To Carl, it all looked faked, but then, he guessed he'd rather have it that way than see women really being tortured. *Did I torture DeeDee? Did I go too far?* He couldn't imagine ending up like these characters, yet they had seemed to be well on their way before he called a temporary halt to it. That was what was bugging him, Carl realized. When he told DeeDee he thought they should take a break so he could be with the "real her," deep down, his id was planning the next conquest of his submissive little girl.

Shaking his head, Carl went to the bar and caught the attention of the bartender. When he came over, Carl shouted over the screaming guitar and pounding drums, "I'm looking for a man who calls himself Master Turk." The bartender put his hand behind his ear, indicating he couldn't hear.

"Master Turk," Carl shouted, feeling like he was standing next to a jet engine. "Do you know him?"

He looked puzzled for a moment then held up one finger. Carl watched as he went down to the other end of the bar and talked into the ear of a raven-haired woman. She looked up sharply at Carl. He smiled, trying to look innocent.

She signaled him to follow her. As he did, he couldn't help but notice how tall she was—nearly as tall as Carl himself. She also seemed quite well-built, with broad shoulders, although she still had a very feminine shape to her. She led him into a corridor, then into a back room. The band noise diminished significantly when she closed the door. Carl's ears rang. She leaned back against it and folded her arms. Carl turned. Across the room, behind a desk sat a huge man, probably weighing close to three hundred pounds. His shiny bald head was dotted with sweat. On the desk, he'd been counting piles of dirty bills. Carl could see a lot of fifties and hundreds. The man lurched to his feet.

"What the fuck is this?"

Carl looked from him to the woman. Before he could speak, she said, "He's looking for Turk."

Baldy grunted. "Oh, yeah? What's your name?"

"Carl." He didn't want to say more.

"What business you got with Turk?" He came over close, invading Carl's space. He stood a good two inches taller. Carl tried not to shrink away.

He chose the "tough guy" route. "Not that it's any of your business, but he told me to look him up when I was in town."

"So you're good buddies, are ya?"

"Not really. We do business together from time to time."

"Oh, really?" He smiled an evil little grin, like he thought that was rich. "You guys do business, but you don't even know which fuckin' club he owns? You must think I'm a fuckin' idiot."

"All right, you got me. He did business with a friend of mine, who got himself killed last year." Carl's mind was racing, trying to come up with a plausible story. "I'm trying to take over his end of the business."

"Yeah? And what business is that?"

"Training slaves," he said without hesitation.

Baldy's narrow eyes widened and he stepped back. "Well, if it's a trainer you want, you couldn't do any better than Mistress Gloria here," he nodded his massive head toward the black-haired woman against the door. Carl turned and had to agree that she looked every bit the Dominatrix.

"Yes, well, I know about the deal my friend and Turk had, so I want to start there. If I don't like the terms, however, I'll come back and see what you might be able to do." Carl tried to sound sincere.

"He's bullshitting you, Hank," Gloria spoke up behind him. "He doesn't know what he's talking about."

"Yeah, I know." Hank smiled like a hangman with his hand on the lever. "You must think I'm some kind of fuckin' chump. You're not a trainer. Get out." He waved at the door.

Carl shrugged, as if it made no difference to him. Yet his mind raced to try and figure out what he'd said wrong. Perhaps it was just his general naïveté. He was resigned to going from club to club until someone pointed him in the right direction.

Gloria followed him out. The noise rose in volume immediately, making Carl wince. When she closed the door behind her, she leaned over suddenly and whispered into his ear above the noise, "For a hundred bucks, I'll tell you where to find Turk."

Time was of the essence. Carl had to get to Turk before he heard someone was searching for him. It was well worth a hundred. He handed her five twenties. She looked around the corridor then tipped her head in the direction of the back door. Carl followed her outside. They were in an alley behind the club. It reeked of stale garbage and was littered with empty beer bottles. At least the noise had mercifully been reduced to a dull throb.

He stood while she checked around, as if afraid to be seen with him. She no longer looked like a dominatrix, more like a spy, fearful of getting caught. "You're not going to kill him, are you?"

"No," he said at once. "I won't kill him."

"Why do you really want him? I know you're not a trainer."

Carl hesitated. "He's got some information I need." He hoped that would satisfy her.

She studied him, as if trying to determine if he could be trusted. "Okay," she finally said, coming close. Carl could smell cigarettes on her breath. "He lives in a mansion on Clairmont Street, right near the intersection with Haight. You can't miss it—it's got stone lions on either side of the gate."

Carl nodded. "Thanks." He started to leave.

"Don't tell him where you got the information." He nodded. She held his arm for another few seconds, her eyes boring into his, then let him go. Without another word, she turned and disappeared back inside. Briefly, the noise assaulted him once again. *It's a wonder they aren't all deaf, working in there.* He turned and headed up the alley.

* * * * *

Mistress Gloria reentered the office, closed the door behind her and leaned against it. She smiled and licked her lips.

"Whadja get?" Hank asked.

"Hunnert. The way he gave it up, I shoulda asked for two. He's a born sucker. You want some of it, Hank?"

Hank shook his head. "Nah. You keep it. I'll get my cut from Turk later." He picked up the phone. "Hey," he said while it rang, "you wanna be cut in on the back end? He might be trainable."

Gloria's smile slowly spread across her face. "Yeah, I think I would."

Chapter Fourteen

Carl found Clairmont Street without trouble then followed it down to Haight Avenue. He parked in the darkness next to a fire hydrant certain he wouldn't be long. For the first time, he wished he'd brought a gun. Coming here without a weapon could be a mistake, despite his self-defense skills. He got out and went to the trunk. Rummaging around, he came across a screwdriver. It would have to do. He slipped it into his belt—point down. He practiced yanking it free, feeling ridiculous. He looked around, afraid someone might see him and alert police—or worse, Turk.

Surprise was his ally. He'd better move fast if he wanted to get the drop on Turk. He crept up the walkway, unsure if he should find an open window and sneak in, or just boldly ring the doorbell, then threaten whoever opened the door. He decided on the latter course because he didn't want to be considered a burglar. No, he was here to rescue DeeDee and nobody better stand in his way.

He rang the bell with his left hand, letting his fingers of his right lightly touch the handle of the screwdriver. When the door opened suddenly, he started forward, his face a snarl, ready to yank out his makeshift weapon, only to stop suddenly, his eyes wide. Instead of Turk, or some evil butler, as he had expected, there stood a slender, delicate Asian woman—a girl, really. She wore a black bustier and leather shorts. She had leather straps around her wrists and ankles, and her slender neck was encircled by a black collar.

"May I help you, Master?" she asked, bowing slightly.

Carl felt suddenly ridiculous. He took his hand off the handle of the screwdriver. "Uh. I'm here to see Turk. I, um, have some business to discuss with him."

"Of course. Please come in. May I take your coat?"

"Er, no, that's all right." Carl pulled the flaps of his windbreaker tighter across his midsection, covering up the handle of his weapon. He hoped she hadn't seen it.

"This way, please. Master Turk is in the study." She pointed to a set of double doors past the huge stairway and began walking ahead of him. Carl dutifully followed behind. He thought it odd that he would be allowed in so easily. Perhaps she had mistaken him for someone else? Mentally, he began to rehearse what he would say to Turk that would convince the man to release DeeDee. Surely, he couldn't believe that tripe that Evers had "bequeathed" her to him!

As he passed the stairway, his mind was still occupied and his eyes were on the Asian girl's swaying bottom. He never noticed the hidden door open beneath the railing to his right. He sensed movement and began to turn in that direction when a spray struck him in the face, getting into his eyes. He screamed, jerking sideways to escape the burning sensation.

"You think you can just walk in here and steal one of MY girls away!" he heard a voice thunder. He wiped at his eyes with his left hand, desperate to clear them, and reached down for his screwdriver with his right. Suddenly he felt a hard fist smash into his head. Carl lurched sideways and went down.

He thought he was unconscious only for a few seconds, but when he woke up, his hands were fastened behind him. He looked down and noticed his feet were tied with plastic cuffs. He struggled to no avail. His eyes still burned, so he couldn't really see his captor. He knew it had to be Turk.

He also knew that he'd been betrayed by Gloria and the bald man. *Damn! What a fool!* He should've known better!

"So, 'Master' Carl," the voice dripped with sarcasm. "I'll bet you've come for your slave."

"She's not a sla—" he started to say, but his voice caught in his throat when Turk kicked him in the leg.

"Silence! I'll tell you when to talk. You're in MY house. Show some respect."

Carl cursed at himself for being so easily captured. He struggled to see Turk's face.

"Crystal, go get a wet cloth. Let's ease our guest's discomfort." He sounded like a warden, concerned about the condemned man's comfort in the electric chair, just before he pulled the switch.

Carl feared he'd been captured by a madman. That he could be in a rage one moment, then giving first aid showed he was unpredictable—the worst kind of tormentor.

Crystal came back with a warm, wet washcloth and wiped the pepper spray out of his eyes. When his vision cleared, he was startled to see Crystal was nude. Gold nipple rings hung from her small breasts. She had no hair between her legs—only a small tattoo on her mons that said "Use Me." He tore his eyes away and squinted up at the looming man above him.

Turk was as DeeDee had described him. Big and beefy with bulging eyes set in a round, fleshy face. He had a thin black beard along his jaw line and his head was bald. But it was his shoulders and upper arms that drew Carl's attention — they were massive. Corded muscles made his neck disappear and he looked like he could toss sacks of cement around all day and not tire. That Carl had thought he could have taken him on with just a screwdriver clearly illustrated his ignorance of the world he had just entered.

"So what do we have here? The white knight?" His laugh was a cruel, throaty vibration. In one hand, he held Carl's wallet. With the other, he held up Carl's screwdriver and shook his head. "You know, we really hate amateurs up here. What'ya think? That you could just stroll in here with this and take away my property?"

"She's not your property — "

"Silence!" He thumped a boot against Carl's ribs. "You know nothing about it. Master Stephen gave her to me before he died, asked me to take care of her."

"He can't do that! She — "

Another kick, harder now, silenced him again.

"He can and he did. If you know anything about DeeDee, you know she likes to be controlled."

Carl risked another kick. "Where have you been for the last year?"

Turk just grunted. "I was busy. But I never forget a promise to an old friend."

"She's changed in a year — Ooff!"

This time, the kick was harder. "Slaves never change, once they've experienced the lifestyle. It's like a drug they can't shake. She needs to be owned. Surely you must've seen it."

Carl had to admit there was something to what he said. DeeDee had fallen right back into her lifestyle with only a little bit of encouragement from him. He'd been attracted to it for a while, fascinated, like a boy with a new toy. Then, just when he'd pulled back and tried to have a more normal relationship with her, Turk had moved in.

"Perhaps you need a little demonstration." He turned and nodded to the Asian girl, who immediately trotted off down the hall. Carl craned his neck to follow her. Crystal came to a bookcase set into the wall and pulled down on one volume. He heard a click and the bookcase popped opened, revealing a passageway behind it. Carl could tell there were stairs there, for she began descending before she disappeared from sight.

Turk leaned down and yanked Carl to a sitting position, scooting him against a wall. His hands felt numb. "Watch and learn," he whispered, his face displaying an evil grin.

In a few minutes, another naked woman appeared in the doorway—DeeDee! Crystal followed right behind. "DeeDee! Thank god you're all..." The words died in his throat. DeeDee's arms were behind her, probably handcuffed. But what really startled him was the change in her appearance. Her makeup was heavier, especially the bright-red lipstick and false eyelashes. She looked like a kewpie doll. She wore a black leather collar around her throat. Similar cuffs surrounded her ankles and probably her wrists as well, though he couldn't see. Gold rings had been replaced in her nipples and he caught a flash of gold between her legs. Turk had taken advantage of DeeDee's piercings. He probably made her wear her master's old jewelry. He heard a slight jingling noise.

She barely glanced at Carl. All her attention was on Turk. She shuffled forward, then quietly kneeled before him, making sure her legs were wide apart. Now Carl could easily see the four gold rings through her labia, two on each side. A tiny silver bell hung from one of the rings. She shook slightly, causing it to tinkle. DeeDee lowered her head and waited.

Turk reached out and cupped her chin, directing her gaze toward Carl. "Look, slave dee," he said softly, like one might talk to a pet. "You've got a visitor. Do you remember Carl?"

Tears came to her eyes. "Yes, Master Turk."

"Carl here says you don't want to be here. He says he's come to 'rescue' you. Do you want to be rescued?"

"No, Master." The voice was rote, wooden.

"You've got her terrified, you bastard! Of course she's going to say—"

With forced casualness, Turk turned and backhanded Carl across the face. He slumped over, unable to break his fall. He tasted blood in his mouth.

"Don't interrupt me again," Turk warned.

He returned to DeeDee. "Now, my new slave, tell Carl why you want to remain here with me."

She turned toward Carl, who was still slumped over, his head touching the floor. "Master Carl, I appreciate everything you've done for me. I won't forget it. But I have a new life with Master Turk now. Please go home."

Using his shoulder blades against the wall, Carl managed to scoot himself partially upright. "Can I ask her a question, Turk?" It killed him to be polite to the bastard.

Turk nodded, seemingly pleased at Carl's respectful tone.

"DeeDee, are you sure this is what Master Stephen would want for you? Wouldn't you rather go home and be with me?"

Turk's eyes narrowed. "That's two questions," he warned, but did not hit him again.

"My home is here," she said simply. "My master gave me to Master Turk, so I will obey him. I owe him that."

Carl wasn't convinced. "You've got her brainwashed," he snarled.

"Oh?" He seemed amused. "Crystal, release her."

Crystal stepped forward and unhooked DeeDee's leather cuffs. DeeDee brought her hands to her sides, but otherwise made no movement.

"Service me," Turk ordered.

DeeDee stood, stepped forward then dropped to her knees again directly in front of Turk. Carl couldn't believe his eyes. She unzipped the big man's pants and gently pulled out his flaccid member. She bent forward, taking his cock into her red-lipped mouth.

Carl might've been convinced that this was what she really wanted out of her life now, except for one thing. As she sucked Turk's cock, Carl could see the track of a tear flowing down from the corner of one eye.

It was all he needed to be convinced. She was a prisoner, and he would save her. Of that, he was determined.

He turned away, not willing to see any more. He listened to the slurping sounds, wishing he could cut off his hearing as easily as he avoided the sight. He sensed

Turk was satisfied that he'd made his point, for the sound soon stopped. Carl looked up to see him gently push DeeDee away and zip up his pants, careful to avoid snagging the zipper on his softening member.

"Not yet convinced? How about this." He turned to Crystal. "Sit on that stool and spread your legs."

She obeyed instantly. She leaned back against the wall, her legs hanging obscenely apart. She closed her eyes.

"Service her," Turk demanded. DeeDee crawled over and fastened her mouth onto Crystal's bare cunt. Carl couldn't help but stare. DeeDee probed with her tongue, eliciting soft noises from Crystal. Turk just stood there, smiling. This went on for several minutes, until Crystal's chin began to bob up and down. Carl could tell she was about to orgasm.

Suddenly, she opened her eyes. "Permission to come, Master?" she asked softly. Her whole body was moving in time with DeeDee's licks.

"Denied." Turk seemed to enjoy the pained expression on his slave's face. He reached out and touched DeeDee on the shoulder and she immediately stopped. She returned to her position of attention. Carl could see the sheen of wetness on her mouth and chin. She seemed completely under Turk's spell.

"See?" he said to Carl, as if the demonstrations had proved his point. To Carl, it had proved the opposite, but he pretended to think otherwise.

"Okay. I was mistaken. I thought DeeDee liked her life with me." He made a show of his disappointment. "I should've known—after all, I've only been going with her a few weeks. If you'll just let me go, I won't bother you again."

For a minute, Turk just stood there, staring at him. Carl tried not to become impatient. He sensed events could go either way. Of course, Turk would be a fool to release him—he'd call the police immediately and Turk would have to explain DeeDee's unusual lifestyle to them. But what other choice was there? Murder? Carl hoped not.

"You must think I'm an idiot," Turk said and Carl tried not to grimace in disappointment. "You'd go straight to the police, like anyone in your position would do. And that might cause me some discomfort. Not that they'd find her here, no. She'd be long gone, sold somewhere or sent out for training."

"You can't keep me here!" Carl barked.

"Don't worry—I have no intention of keeping you. Men aren't my thing; I train only women. I have a better idea. Come, let us go into the library, shall we?" He magnanimously reached down and helped Carl to his feet. Because of the straps around his ankles, he could only bounce alongside the big man, feeling like a fool. Turk ended up dragging him through the door. He noticed that DeeDee and Crystal trailed behind them, like obedient slaves should.

Inside, Carl got another shock. There, in a chair by the cold fireplace, sat Gloria! How had she gotten here so fast? The dark-haired dominatrix was dressed just as she had been at the club—shiny dark leather bustier and black fishnet stockings. She held a black leather riding crop in one hand, slapping it gently into the palm of her other hand.

"You!" he breathed, his anger flaring.

"Yes. Me. Did you think I'd miss out on an opportunity like this?"

Carl was confused. *What the hell was she talking about?*

Turk helped him to a chair, where he sat down heavily. "What the hell's going on? If you don't let me go, you'll be in a lot more trouble than you're already in right now."

"Shut up. You're in no position to speak." Gloria's words stung him.

Carl turned to see Turk walk to a large desk. He tossed Carl's wallet, cell phone and screwdriver onto the blotter and began rummaging through the drawers. Carl craned his head around until he could see DeeDee and begged for help with his eyes. She just stood there, staring at him, her face blank, her lipstick smeared. Her jewelry winked at him in the lights.

He turned back to Gloria. "Okay, so you guys must think I'm a big chump. I come here to help this girl, and you stopped me cold. Now that we've all had our fun, I'd like to be released. If you do, I won't have you all charged with kidnapping."

Both Gloria and Turk laughed, as if sharing a private joke. Carl didn't like the way this was going. Turk returned from the desk, holding up a syringe that he poked into a small vial of clear liquid. Carl watched, horrified, as Turk drew a few cc's into the syringe.

"No! What the hell is that?! Get away from me!" He couldn't stop the panic in his voice. He was sure he was about to be killed.

"Relax," Turk said, as he approached him. "This is just something to make you sleep. So you won't cause any trouble during your journey."

"Journey?! What journey?! Where are you taking me?! I demand to be released!"

Turk pinched Carl's upper arm and effortlessly jabbed the needle home. He could feel the warm solution enter his veins. His arm grew numb then the feeling began to spread throughout his body.

His eyesight grew dim. He heard Turk tell Gloria. "He's all yours."

"Thanks," she replied, standing up. "I could use another slave in my little dungeon."

His world faded to black.

Chapter Fifteen

Carl awoke groggily. He struggled to focus his eyes. His first thought was, *I'm glad I'm not dead.* His second thought: *Shit—I'm naked.* He shivered in the cool air.

He was in a small cell, about four feet wide and seven feet deep. It had bars on the top and sides. The floor was cement. He was lying on a small cot. The only other fixture was a metal toilet, with a one-tap sink above it. He had to crane his neck to see it, for he couldn't get up. Both his wrists were held close to his body, attached to a large leather strap that encircled his waist. He peered down and noticed his ankles were also chained, restricting his movements.

He shifted his gaze to the room beyond the bars. It seemed to be a basement of some kind. Though it was dimly lit, he estimated it measured about fifteen by twenty-five feet. Rafters ran along the ceiling, presumably holding up the floor of the house above him. Stairs ran up into darkness along the far wall. The walls were old stone jumbled together and held by mortar. He guessed it was a turn-of-the-century house. Turning to his left, he saw another identical cell, empty.

He could still be in San Francisco, he thought. Or he could've been out for hours and now might be anywhere in the world. He'd have to listen carefully for clues. That he would escape, he had no doubt. It was just a matter of time, waiting for the right opportunity.

His bladder ached. He had to pee. "Hey!" he shouted.

He lay there, twitching and struggling against his bonds for what seemed like another hour before he heard the thud-clank of the door above him. That told him it was a thick wooden door, reinforced by steel. He was determined to memorize every clue.

The thump of feet on the stairs caused him to try to sit up, but a collar around his throat held him down. It appeared to be attached to the cot by a short length of chain.

"Hey!" He shouted again. "Let me go!"

Gloria came into view, followed by a tall, well-muscled blond man, naked except for a loincloth. She had on a different outfit — thigh-high black boots under a black leather coat, unbuttoned down the middle. A red bustier winked at him from between the flaps. In her hand, she carried her ubiquitous riding crop. It was like something out of a bad movie. He laughed in spite of his predicament. "What the hell is this? Frankenstein? Or Barbarella?"

She came to the cell, jangling some skeleton keys in her free hand. She just stood there, watching him. Carl waited as long as he could, considering his bladder was about to burst, then said, "Come on! I gotta pee!"

"Your first lesson," she responded. "You are to call me 'Mistress'. Can you remember that?"

If he hadn't been on the verge of wetting himself, Carl might've told her to go fuck herself. But he sensed that arguing with her right now would be counterproductive. "All right, Mistress. Please release me so I can pee — unless you want me to soil your nice bed here."

Gloria opened the door. The big blond man came in behind her, no doubt backing her up. *Good thing*, he thought. *If she unlocked me without the muscle, I'd probably kill her.* Carl could feel his rage building. He knew he could take down the blond man. He prepared to launch himself at him once he was freed.

She leaned over and unclipped the chain from between his ankles, then came forward to release the chain on his collar. Carl sat up immediately glad to be in a different position. He waited until she unlocked his hands, but she made no move to do so.

He wiggled his fingers by his hips. "Hey. What about my hands?" He quickly added, "Mistress."

"You don't need your hands." She turned to the blond man and nodded. "Sven will help you."

"Help me pee? Oh, come on, I don't swing that way."

She laughed. "You aren't supposed to enjoy it. It's just that you aren't, um, trustworthy enough to have your hands released right now."

"Well, why don't you help me?" Carl hoped maybe he could make her let down her guard with his charm. He felt his chance slipping away.

In response, she cracked the riding crop across his thigh. "Yeouch!" he yelped.

"You are not to question my decisions. That's lesson two." She locked her eyes with his.

The ludicrousness of the situation kept him from losing his temper. *Pee first, then kill.* "Yes, ma'am."

Again, the riding crop struck him, this time on the other thigh. "Ouch! Dammit!"

"What is my name?"

"Mistress! Mistress Gloria!" *Hell*, he thought, *what's wrong with 'ma'am'?*

"Very well. You may stand and approach the toilet."

Carl did so, trying to ignore the throbbing in both legs. He shuffled to the toilet, aware of Sven right behind him. The blond man pressed up tight against his backside, his left hand reaching around to rest on Carl's stomach, giving him the creeps. But he really shuddered when Sven brought his right hand around and gently took Carl's soft cock in hand. Sven aimed it at the water.

Carl didn't think he could release now. His muscles froze.

"You'd better take advantage of this opportunity because it's the only way you're going to be allowed to pee," she said. He sensed she was moving away, perhaps to give him a little space. But it wasn't her that he was worried about. Sven seemed like the kind of guy who could swing either way and he didn't want to encourage him.

Finally, he relaxed his muscles enough to let the first dribble of water come out. Sven adjusted his aim to the center of the toilet. Soon, the dribble became a stream and he began to feel better.

"That wasn't so hard, was it?" Gloria's voice came from outside the cell, to Carl's left, and he couldn't help but turn in that direction. There came a sudden flash of light and he blinked in surprise. *A camera!* Despite the spots in his eyes, he could see Gloria, standing there with a Polaroid.

He felt Sven press his stomach tighter, encouraging him not to move, while the stream began to fade. Another flash caught him in this embarrassing position and he felt violated and enraged.

"Dammit!" He said under his breath.

His stream petered out and Sven dutifully shook his cock for him and stepped aside. Carl wanted to kick him, but held off. He really wanted to kick Gloria, even if it meant falling down. He waited until the so-called Mistress began to re-enter the cell, then took a step forward, getting his right leg ready to kick her right in the stomach. Suddenly, Sven pushed him hard, and Carl fell heavily onto the cot, banging his head against the bars.

"Ow!"

Gloria bent down, her face close. "Don't ever think of attacking me. Sven is very protective of me." While he was helpless, he could feel Sven reattaching the chain between his ankles, preventing any further leg movement.

She crouched down and admired two Polaroids. Carl could only see the backs. "Rather nice, if I do say so myself. Looks like you're enjoying yourself a little bit too." She turned them and Carl could see himself being held by the tall Swede, his cock in the man's hand, his face relaxing from the release of urine. But it also might look like a man who was enjoying the attention of another man.

"That's not…right," he said lamely. "You make it look like I'm gay or something." He remembered the old line from "Seinfeld". "Not that there's anything wrong with that. I just don't, er, do that."

Gloria cupped his chin in her soft hand and tipped his face up to hers. "By the time I'm finished with you, sweetheart, you won't care one way or another. You'll do what you're told."

Carl got a sinking feeling. "You can't possibly plan to keep me here!"

"Oh, yes. And while you're here, your old girlfriend is being trained to accept whatever Turk—or any owner—

wants, not that that will take much doing." She paused then laughed, a deep throaty contralto. "Maybe when we're both done, you two can provide an evening's entertainment for the Masters and Mistresses."

Carl thrashed in his bonds, hearing the laughter echoing in his head.

Chapter Sixteen

Carl could tell that Gloria was experienced at training men, but he suspected they might be inclined in that direction already. He knew there were men who liked to be dominated—abused, even. But he couldn't imagine that she could take a strong-willed man and break him down until he acted like the silent Swede. Sven must have wanted to be a mindless drone, otherwise, he could've stopped Gloria anytime.

He wondered if he might establish some sort of rapport with him. If Sven would just give him an opening, he could escape. But that would ruin Sven's carefully constructed world, wouldn't it? No, he'd better not count on him.

They had left him, shivering on the cot, chained the way he had been before. He expected the bleak environment and the chains were necessary to make him feel alone and helpless. Later, Gloria would begin the reward and punishment phase. Somewhere along in there, he might have to fake submission, so he could get her to trust him. Once she freed him from his chains, well, then, look out, bitch.

For now, he'd have to play along. He'd never paid much attention to this seamy underworld. He knew there were clubs for slaves and masters, yet he'd never been interested in them—until he'd meet DeeDee. Hell, he might've been drawn into it because of her. She made him feel, well, masterful. Like he could do no wrong.

Even when he had shaken himself out of it and tried to treat DeeDee like a normal girl, he felt, in the back of his mind, that he might want to return to the lifestyle sometimes. Perhaps just as a lark to spice up their relationship. She never seemed so sexy as when she was calling him master and obeying his every whim.

Still, it was a lot of power to give someone. Sure, Carl reasoned, he was at least decent enough not to take full advantage of her proclivities. He was a mere dabbler compared to someone like Turk. Or Evers. Carl couldn't understand why Evers would "bequeath" DeeDee to a man like Turk. He believed, from what she had told him, that Evers dabbled in the lifestyle. But Turk lived the life daily. He was the dark side to the master/slave game. Evers should have known that turning DeeDee over to Turk would've ruined her for a normal life. Why would he do that?

Carl could only imagine what she must be going through right now. Any independent thoughts would be flushed out until she was just a vessel for Turk's dark visions. The DeeDee he knew would be gone forever — if he couldn't get to her soon. Very soon.

He wondered how he'd got himself into this mess. He considered himself an ordinary guy, working a normal job and dating normal women. When he'd first met DeeDee, he thought she was beautiful, but never expected what lay behind her façade. When he did, he had felt blessed. *Heck*, he thought, *who wouldn't?*

Now he felt cursed by it.

"DeeDee, I wish you'd just put on the damn underwear in high school!" he said aloud, then immediately bit his lip, fearing Gloria was listening and watching somehow. Wasn't that the way it worked? The "masters" spied on their slaves so they could better control them?

Carl looked around, trying to spot cameras but found none. "Probably hidden," he muttered under his breath.

* * * * *

"You don't really expect to break him, do you?" Mistress Abigail asked Gloria as they sat on the couch in the spacious living room upstairs. "I mean, he doesn't seem trainable, if you ask me." Abigail was dressed in a simple tank top and red leather skirt, her legs splayed wide apart to give the man's head between them more room.

Gloria took a sip of her wine and nodded to her friend. She had known Abigail for eight years now, ever since they met at a BDSM nightclub, male slaves in tow on leashes. They had taken one look at each other and burst out laughing; they'd been friends ever since.

"No, probably not. He has the look of a hunter, don't you think?" she responded, pointing to the large TV screen that showed Carl in his cell, tied to the cot. "But I just couldn't resist the effort, you know?"

"Oh, I know, trust me," Abigail agreed, adjusting her legs. "Oooh, Brian, that's nice." Brian, of course, made no comment. His tongue was too busy for speech.

"He's rather new, isn't he?" Gloria asked, waving her wineglass at the energetic slave serving his mistress. Like Sven, he was dressed solely in a loincloth.

"Yes, I've had him about six months now. Got him from Jen in San Francisco. She grew tired of him and wanted to find a nice home for him."

"Looks like he found it," Gloria grinned. "I'll bet he spends a lot of time there."

"Ohh!" Abigail nearly lifted out of her seat. "Goodness! Yes, he's one of the best I've had. And his cock is pretty good, too."

"Can I see?" Gloria hoped it was hard. She loved holding a man's hard cock in her hand.

"Of course. Brian," Abigail tapped him on the head. "Take a break and go show Mistress Gloria your cock." She sat up a little straighter.

Immediately, Brian rose, the juices from Abigail's pussy on his face and came over to Gloria. She took in his muscular chest and six-pack abs before dropping her gaze. She could see he was excited—his loincloth couldn't hide his bulging member. He flipped it up for her as he stood, just outside her knees, and waited for instructions.

Gloria leaned over and gripped it gently, mentally comparing it to Sven's. It was a healthy seven inches, about the same as her slave's. However, that gave her an idea.

"Sven, come over here." The Swede dutifully approached. His loincloth, however, sagged limply. "Get yourself hard, I want to compare you two."

Sven stood next to Brian, reached under his loincloth and began stroking his cock. This seemed to have an unfortunate effect on Brian—his hard cock began to wither. Gloria immediately began stroking it, causing it to return to its full glory.

Now Abigail got into the act. She slid over on the couch and pressed her face next to Gloria's shoulder, taking in the action. Her face was rapt, her mouth slightly open. "There's just nothing like a man's hard cock, is there?" she said dreamily.

"No, although you know I like my girls."

That was certainly true. While Abigail preferred to train male slaves exclusively, Gloria reveled in her bisexuality. Besides Carl, she had another wing of her "dungeon" that contained two female slaves she was currently training. One for herself and another for a friend.

Sven's cock was nearly fully extended now. Gloria made the men stand hip to hip and compared them. They were about the same length and thickness. The most obvious difference: Brian's cock was circumcised, while Sven still had his thick foreskin. It hadn't bothered Gloria before, but now she wasn't so sure.

"What do you think of his foreskin?" she asked Abigail.

"Well, you know me. I like 'em undressed. Otherwise, it's like making love to a man in a turtleneck."

Gloria laughed, but it got her to thinking. Perhaps she could have the offending skin removed. "The operation's not all that difficult for an adult, is it?"

Her words, more thoughts spoken out loud than a question for Abigail, caused Sven's cock to deflate at once. Both women laughed again. "Oh, Sven, don't worry. I'm only talking about it. I'm not sure it's something I need to do."

But the seed was planted in her mind and Sven probably knew it. His cock hung limply between his legs.

It irritated Gloria and she knew just what would fix it. "Sven," she barked, "service me." She spread her legs.

Abigail snapped her fingers at Brian and moved back to her former position on the couch. He dove back underneath her short red skirt and started licking her anew.

Sven dropped down to his knees and carefully unfastened the lower part of his mistress's bustier and moved it out of the way, exposing her naked loins to him. He dipped down and ran his tongue lightly across the closed slit, just as he'd been trained to do.

Thanks to his mistress's careful training, Sven could make love to a woman for hours, beginning with his touch on her sensitive skin, then using his lips and tongue in all her erogenous zones until she was a puddle of muscle and flesh, her bones poking through her skin. Only then would he tease his hard cock into her sopping wet canal to bring her to new heights of pleasure. The man was a dream.

Gloria let Sven's tongue work its magic while her mind drifted to the problem of this Carl fellow. She didn't want the intrusion, she just couldn't help it—she had taken Carl because Turk probably would've killed him. She didn't have that meanness within her, thank god. She was a lover, not a fighter, although she didn't hesitate to use whatever means necessary to train her slaves.

But that brought her back to Carl's innate character. Not all men were like Sven and Brian, of that she was very clear. Turning Carl into a pleasure slave might not be possible. Then what? Send him back to Turk to be killed? Wouldn't that just make her an accomplice to murder?

Sven's gentle tongue worked home, bringing her mind back to the present. She could feel her clit sigh and extend like a reluctant maiden. Gloria noted she was still a bit tender from their energetic session last night—having a new slave in her dungeon always made her horny and she had taken it out on her trusty Sven. Now she wanted Sven to slow down. She reached up and pushed down the demi-cups of her bustier.

"Sven," she said. "Nipples."

Immediately, Sven moved up over her stomach to attach his soft, pulpy lips onto her right nipple. He nibbled and sucked for a few minutes until it extended to its full length, then he moved to the left.

Gloria marveled at how well Sven knew her body. He was so well-trained, he could sense her needs with a touch or a word, always bringing her to orgasm after orgasm. She was never going to let this man go.

She found her mind wandering again, to the first time Sven came to be her slave. He had been a raw immigrant, working as a bouncer in one of Hank's clubs. She could tell right away he wasn't a fighter. He'd been drawn to the lifestyle because he couldn't help himself, and took the first job that was offered. He was a lousy bouncer; that much became evident.

When Hank threatened to fire him, Gloria had stepped in and "suggested" he come stay with her for a while. He had accepted gratefully, not knowing that they were both embarking on a symbiotic relationship.

It had started out innocently enough. Since Gloria didn't charge him rent, he had to work it off somehow, she told him. She began by making him sweep up, cook dinners and draw her baths. All the while, she teased him with the possibility that he'd get laid in the end, though she didn't give in. Yes, he could've forced himself on her, but he never did, out of respect for her and realizing the power she had over him.

She used that power to push him further and further along toward slavery, without his even being fully aware of it. Of course, she suspected this was what he had really wanted all along. It was more of a game they played. She would exert more control over him and he would acquiesce, bobbing his head in submission.

Soon, she had him vacuuming her home dressed only in an apron, his cock pressing against the flimsy material. Something about a man doing household chores naked or nearly so really turned her on—she couldn't explain it.

He was a highly sexual creature, so Gloria could use the carrot of her body against the stick of "punishments" for disobedience. The punishments were usually slaps on his bare bottom, but it was enough to correct this thinking. His main motivation was the promise that she might give in to him, if he behaved himself.

That's how she got him to wear the collar and cuffs. She had explained that because he was so much bigger and stronger than she was, she needed a way to control him. Otherwise, she wouldn't feel comfortable having him in her home. He readily agreed—anything to stay a while longer in her presence, to perhaps one day explore the pleasures of her flesh.

Gloria then attached a leash to his collar and led him around, getting him used to being under her control. He didn't seem to mind, especially when she wore short skirts that flashed her ass at him while they walked.

Her body proved to be a powerful weapon to further his obedience. Her favorite training method was to chain him by his collar to the wall then slowly strip just out of his reach, displaying her body to him and promising the delights to come. After that, he seemed eager to learn.

The first time she let him touch her was only with his hands cuffed behind his back. He lay on the bed, squirming over his hard-on, while she teased him just out of reach, making him watch her undress. When she pulled her panties off, she knew he was ready to please her—his tongue was already out, licking his upper lip. Gloria had kept her riding crop handy as she scooted closer to his face, telling him he had to do exactly what she told him to do, or he'd feel the lash of the leather.

Within a few weeks, she had him tongue-trained to bring her to multiple orgasms. A month after that, she allowed him to fuck her for the first time—but only on her terms. He had to stroke her, caress her, encourage her and bring her to several orgasms for an hour or more before she would allow him to enter her.

What a woman wouldn't pay for man like that! Not that she'd ever sell him. She had hoped Carl could be trained, but she was beginning to have her doubts. He seemed too wild and too much in control at the same time. Some men were just like that. Perhaps she could start his training then sell him to someone overseas. Someone with more severe training techniques. Yes, that might work.

The orgasm began to build, drawing her attention away from the problem downstairs and back onto Sven's insistent tongue. She rode it like a surfer toward a shining goal. In seconds, she was shuddering with relief.

Next to her, Gloria could hear Abigail approaching her own orgasm, her voice rising in octaves. *Ahh, this was the life*, Gloria mused. *Why couldn't all women live this way?*

Chapter Seventeen

DeeDee huddled in her cell, dried tears on her face. She had wept after Carl had been taken away, but only after she had been returned to the dungeon. She dared not show her tears to Master Turk. The one tear that had fallen while she was fellating him she had managed to wipe away before he'd noticed.

Now, hours later, she tried to sort out her thoughts. She had enjoyed her life with Master Stephen. He had awakened this need within her that, on one level, took control of her life. But somehow, it was always a game. She felt she could stop anytime just by putting on underwear. It was like their safe word. When Stephen died, she thought she had been ready to let that lifestyle die with him.

Dating Charlie, then Frank may not have been the wisest choices for boyfriends after Stephen, but at least it had given her a look at traditional male-female relationships. After all, she'd been with Stephen since college.

When Carl walked into her life, DeeDee had thought he'd be like the others. Yet he turned out to be a quiet Dom. His approach had been much like Master Stephen's—take it slow, use it as a sexual stimulant, and above all, have fun. She had trusted Carl and would've gladly continued the experiment if he hadn't gotten cold feet.

But Turk? He was entirely different. DeeDee couldn't understand why her former master had thought she needed to be under the control of a man like Turk. She felt betrayed. Turk didn't love her as Stephen had. She was a mere collectible. A valuable item to be trained, then sold.

At least Turk hadn't raped her. Yet. He appeared to have no sexual interest in her, yet he wanted to make sure she'd offer herself to whomever he chose. So far, she'd endured only punishments meant to break her spirit. She knew that the time would come soon when she would be forced to satisfy a man by fucking him. She dreaded that encounter. She also knew, when the time came, she would obey without question. In a perverse way, this was exactly what she'd been trained to do. The game was becoming reality.

She wondered what had happened to Carl. She had gathered that he had been turned over to Gloria for "training", but that could've been a euphemism for murder. The last she had seen of her boyfriend was when they wheeled him out in a large steamer trunk, neatly packed in. She'd noticed several breathing holes, but that meant little. They would be ideal for letting water in, for example, had they stopped at the nearest bridge to dump him over.

DeeDee tried not to think about things like that. She still had hope, however forlorn, that he might return for her. He had seemed to say otherwise, but she suspected he had been talking just for Turk's benefit. She couldn't imagine Carl would just abandon her—would he? *No, if he can, he'll be back*, she decided. *Unless he's already dead.*

Her thoughts were interrupted by the sound of the door opening at the top of the stairs. She looked over, waiting with expectation and dread. Master Turk came thumping down the stairs, followed, as usual, by a nude Crystal. He padded softly across the carpet to stand outside her cell. He put a large key in the lock as he spoke.

"Good afternoon, my pet. I apologize for not appearing earlier. I've been remiss in your training."

He stepped back and allowed her to exit. Crystal stood to one side. DeeDee followed Turk to the center of the room. When he turned back to her, she dropped down to her knees without a word, her legs apart, eyes down.

"So well-trained. I like that. I know Master Stephen awakened the slave within you, which is why you are here today. But he wasn't a true master. More of a dilettante, I'd say. Which was fine as far as it goes, but you need to experience the true meaning of slavery. You need to give yourself over completely to your master."

As DeeDee listened, a chill settled around her heart. She was well on her way to becoming a true slut, ready to be used and abused by men. Her life with Carl—or Stephen for that matter—would seem like a harmless parlor game compared to the life she was about to live. Her only hope was that she would be bought by a man with some kindness in him. It was a slim hope, but it was all she had.

He signaled for her to rise, then escorted her to the post in the center of the room. DeeDee knew what this meant. She didn't know what she had done wrong. Why was he treating her this way? Hadn't she already shown her obedience?

As he slipped her delicate hands into the manacles, he whispered, "Do not fret, my pet. You are too valuable to be permanently damaged. But you need to explore your limits before you can be called a true sex slave."

He turned her to face the post, then stepped back and nodded at Crystal. She flipped a switch, causing the steel cable connected to the manacles to rise up toward a pulley at the top of the post. In seconds, DeeDee found herself on her tiptoes. The whine of the winch stopped then reversed, giving her a little more footing. Her naked breasts brushed the smooth surface of the post, polished, no doubt, by the oils and tears of countless slaves before her. She felt her nipples extend in fear, the gold rings seemed to burn in them.

She looked over her shoulder as Turk retrieved a flat strap from the wall. She shuddered to think he planned to use it on her. "Please, Master," she begged. "I'll be good."

Turk ignored her. He positioned himself, then reared back and struck her. The strap slapped against her pale bottom, causing a flash of pain. She cried out. In seconds, the pain faded, leaving only a heat that spread throughout her back and loins. He struck her again and again, each time moving the target from her hips down to her thighs.

DeeDee was surprised at her reaction. With each blow, she cried out from the sudden pain, but as it faded, she felt an incredible heat that seemed to concentrate on her pussy. She couldn't understand it.

Turk stopped after six blows and returned the strap to its position on the wall. He approached the sobbing woman and caressed her back and shoulders, careful not to touch her tender ass.

"There, my sweet. Sometimes, a slave needs a beating. Not for anything you did, but to show you your place in this world. I know that's something your former master failed to do regularly."

He turned for a moment and DeeDee heard the winch and felt her arms relaxing. When her hands were about chest-high, the winch stopped. Turk handed her an index card, which she couldn't read at first because tears clouded her eyes.

"Relax, my dear. Wipe away your tears. When you can see, I want you to read this card aloud." DeeDee saw Crystal approach with a small object. When she neared, DeeDee could tell it was a tape recorder. She blinked away her tears, then began reading the card.

"I am a slave. My body, my mouth, my cunt and my ass belong to my Master or Mistress. I exist only to give them pleasure. If I fail to instantly obey any command, I must be punished. If my master wishes to punish me for any reason or for no reason at all, it is my duty to bear it. Use me, Master. Use me, Mistress. I beg you."

Though she was frightened, DeeDee read the words without a slip the first time. Turk congratulated her. He unlocked her wrists. "Service me," he barked.

DeeDee dropped to her knees on the carpet and fumbled to unzip her master's pants. She was careful not to snag the bulging penis within on the edge of the zipper as she freed it. Then she opened her mouth to accept the monster and tried to bring him pleasure. She had no other thoughts in her mind. Her sore ass and thighs reminded her to obey. It took her several minutes, but she finally brought him to a climax. She managed to swallow his seed, though it tasted bitter in her mouth.

Later, when they put her back in her cell, Crystal set up the tape recorder just outside and attached it to speakers. The tape played in a loop, so she could hear her own words over and over, mocking her, defining her: "I am a slave. My body, my mouth, my cunt and my ass belong to my Master or Mistress…"

Chapter Eighteen

Carl stood against the post, his hands manacled behind it, a leather strap holding his waist against the rough surface. His feet were chained to the base as well, keeping him helpless. He stared at Gloria, as if he could burn a hole in her. For the moment, he ignored Sven, standing just behind her.

She laughed lightly, as if amused by his anger. "Tut, tut, my slave," she said, approaching him and tapping his cheek with the riding crop. "You must learn to cooperate with your master or mistress."

She caught the narrowing of his eyes. "Oh, yes. You may be purchased by a master. We have quite a need in San Francisco for well-trained male slaves, if you know what I mean." She giggled. "But I can see it in your eyes, 'Oh, Mistresses, I don't swing that way'," she mocked him with a high-pitched voice. "You'd be surprised what my slaves can get used to. Heck, you might even enjoy it."

Gloria turned to Sven. "Take Sven here. When he came to me, he preferred only women too. Didn't you, dear?" The big blond man nodded. "But I've convinced him to enjoy both sexes. Here, I'll show you. Sven." She pointed at Carl's flaccid cock, hanging vulnerably between his legs.

Sven stepped forward then dropped to his knees in front of the bound man. Carl reacted violently when he saw what the man was up to. He thrashed in his bonds, tried to kick his feet loose of their chains. All to no avail.

Sven opened his mouth and took Carl's cock into it, licking it, stroking it gently. Carl tried to pull back or move sideways, but Sven wouldn't let him dislodge himself from the man's mouth.

"Dammit!" Carl exploded. "I'll get you for this, you bitch!"

Gloria continued to smile, but it had become frozen. Carl hoped that was a sign that things weren't working out as planned for her. Surely she had to know that this would be a big waste of time!

Even as Sven slurped at him, Carl tried to concentrate on escape. He had to save DeeDee. He figured he could make it very unpleasant for Gloria to train him, but that would take too much time—not to mention be very painful. He wasn't sure if he would survive it.

He had to find an opportunity—and soon. But would she make a mistake? Or could he create an opportunity?

Carl continued to struggle, even as his cock began to respond to Sven's tongue. After all, a mouth is a mouth, right? A weaker personality might just relax and let the feelings happen, pretend it's a woman down there.

His cock swelled, then faded, then swelled again. Carl fought it all the way, as if his life depended on it. But it wasn't his life he was defending, it was his freedom. He wondered how DeeDee could enjoy being someone's slave. Had he been forcing her to his will, like Gloria was trying to do to him now? He felt shame for his treatment of DeeDee. She had seemed to like it, but he probably went too far in the mall when he put her on display. Still, she had responded enthusiastically in bed later. His mind was in turmoil.

Dammit! If he could just escape! His thoughts returned to his cock. He stopped struggling and let Sven's talented mouth do its magic. Soon, his cock was fully erect and he believed he could come—as long as he didn't look down. If he kept his eyes closed, he could pretend it was DeeDee sucking at him.

Sven licked and sucked until Carl felt himself on the verge of coming. *Go ahead,* his mind told him, *allow yourself this simple pleasure.* But just when he thought he might come, Gloria stepped up and put her hand on Sven's shoulder. He stopped immediately and pulled back.

Carl opened his eyes and locked his with Gloria's. "See, my pet," she said, stroking his erect member lightly, "you can enjoy the pleasures of another man. If I chose to, I could sell you to a man in San Francisco who would very much appreciate someone like you under his control. He'd have to be a strong man, of course. With sufficient training, you could learn to give head as well as receive it."

Carl's cock ached for release in her hand.

"Aaaah, look, you're still hard from a man's mouth and it's just your first lesson. And we have many weeks of training ahead. Already your body betrays you. Soon your mind will follow. You will learn. You will suck when I tell you to suck, you will caress whoever I tell you to and you will instantly obey any command."

She stared back at Carl. "I can see your defiance. That's okay. Many of my subjects were defiant in the beginning. Sven included. But trust me—I have ways of making you change your mind."

Carl jerked in his bonds and growled at her, letting the red haze of his anger flash before bringing it under control. He'd need all his control if he was to escape this madwoman and her twisted lifestyle.

His cock shrank. Gloria released it, then stepped even closer, until her lips were just inches from his. "Looks like you need a little lesson in obedience," she said, then rapped the side of his jaw with the riding crop. Carl winced, though it didn't hurt much.

"Ohh, what's this? Did that hurt? Well, perhaps we've found your weakness. Every man has one. Sven!"

She stepped back and her slave came forward immediately. "Let's give our new slave his first taste of the lash, shall we?"

She laughed at Carl's expression. "But let's be careful, dear. Don't give him a chance to get loose."

Sven didn't. He left the chains to his feet in place and the strap holding Carl's waist tight to the post while he unfastened one of the cuffs around his wrists. Carl tried to swing at him with his free hand, but couldn't get any purchase. Sven's big hand trapped it easily and brought it around to the front and refastened the handcuffs. He attached the cuffs to a steel cable that ran up to the top of the pole, then went to the wall. Carl could see a large wheel there. Sven turned it, drawing Carl's bound hands up to just above his head.

Sven returned, loosened the waist strap, then bent down and unhooked one chain. He brought that leg behind his other one and refastened it, causing Carl to stand awkwardly like a crane. He wasn't sure what this was supposed to accomplish until Sven stood and unhooked the strap around his waist. Now Carl understood. Sven meant to turn him around, facing the post.

Sven grabbed his hips and rotated them, causing his feet to become untangled. He was helpless to stop him with his hands over head. In seconds, Carl's waist was reconnected to the post. All he could see was the grain of the wood in front of him. He twisted around in time to see Sven pull on the wheel, drawing Carl's hands further up the post.

He mocked himself. *Good. My plan is working perfectly!* Then he cursed silently at his predicament. He heard Gloria select a weapon of choice and waited for the first blow.

He sensed Gloria approaching and tried not to tense up. She leaned in to whisper in his ear. "The sooner you cooperate, the sooner the punishments can stop," she told him then she was gone.

He heard the whistling of something deadly and when it struck him, he thought he might die from the shock and the pain. He cried out in spite of himself, all thoughts of being stoic dissipating like smoke in the wind.

Another blow struck him, pressing him against the post and forcing another cry from his lips. The red haze of fury now obscured his vision and he felt out of control. He struggled to rein in his emotions, knowing he had to play this just right or be lost, perhaps forever.

Tears streamed from his face as blows three and four struck. He screamed, begging her to stop. Each successive blow hurt, but somehow he had become numb — or maybe his mind was finally taking control. He hoped he sounded convincing. She had beaten many a man, after all. She might see through his charade.

When the seventh blow struck, Carl yelped then sagged in his bonds, feigning unconsciousness. He could feel blood trickling down his back. Now everything hinged on his ability to convince Gloria and Sven that he was truly out. He let his head loll, his mouth hung open, drooling.

He heard Gloria approach and felt her poke his ribs with her riding crop. He made no movement.

"Looks like our big brave hero can't stand a little discipline, huh, Sven?"

There was silence for a moment then the riding crop slashed down across his spine. The pain flashed anew in his head, but he willed himself not to react. He had expected some treachery like that. He concentrated on DeeDee. *I have to save DeeDee!*

"Better cut him down and put him in his cell. On his stomach, of course. Make sure his hands and feet are cuffed—we don't want to give him any chance to escape. Then you can put some salve on his wounds."

Carl felt the cable lengthen and his hands came down. He let his body sag along with it, scraping painfully against the post. His feet were still chained to the base, so he hung awkwardly, his head between his arms.

He felt Sven at his feet, unchaining him from the post. Sven grabbed Carl around the waist and reached up with his left hand to unhook his cuffs from the cable. Carl let himself sag into the man's arms. Sven was in an awkward position himself at the moment and Carl took full advantage of it. He stepped out with his right foot and pivoted, bringing both his bound hands up in a double fist, catching the bigger man right under the chin. Sven grunted and let him go, spinning away.

Carl followed him, ignoring the woman for the moment, and front-kicked him in the stomach just as he spun to face him. Sven buckled. His head came down and Carl drove his knee up into his face. There came a nasty crunching sound and Sven collapsed onto the concrete floor.

"Bastard!"

Carl spun and dodged just in time to avoid a desperate Gloria from beaning him over the head with a wooden club. As her right arm rushed past, he grabbed her wrist with both hands then used his left elbow to press against her elbow backwards to force her to the floor. She was a strong woman, and he had to press until he heard her bones creak before she went all the way down.

"Do what I say or I'll break your arm," he growled. He stood, hunched over, and dragged her along with him to Sven, who was groaning, holding his bloody face. It was awkward trying to get the keys, so he had to let Gloria go while he uncuffed his wrists. He backhanded her across her face. "Don't move or I'll hurt you," he warned.

He quickly put the cuffs on Sven. Gloria stayed on her stomach, watching him warily, her face a mask of concern for Sven.

While the big man was still semiconscious, he dragged him over to a cell and tossed him onto the cot, then locked the door. He heard a noise, turned and saw Gloria up and running for the basement door.

He sprinted after her, knowing that if she reached the door before he did, he'd be trapped down there. He didn't have time for that, not if he was going to get to DeeDee in time.

He caught her halfway up the stairs. He reached up and locked an arm around her throat from behind, then dragged her kicking and screaming back down the stairs and over to the second cell. She was strong and managed to kick him with her heel between his legs. He grimaced and tightened his grip on her throat until she began to sag. Then he pushed her into the cell and slammed the door on her face.

She recovered quickly. "You can't leave us here!" she shouted. "Sven needs medical attention. Look what you did!" She pointed at the groaning Swede.

"Yeah?" he responded, half turning his back to her. "Look what you did. I'd say we're even."

"But we'll starve down here!"

"You're not getting out until I get DeeDee out. So you'd better hope I succeed. If he kills me, you *will* starve."

"No! You bastard!" Then, like a light switch, she changed her tone. "Wait! Carl! Let me help you! I can distract Turk while you save the girl! I promise I'll help!"

Carl had to laugh. "You think I'd trust you? You're crazier than I thought."

"You don't understand! I saved you! Turk would've killed you! I took you even though I didn't think you were trainable, just to save your life."

That stopped Carl. He didn't want to believe her, but he imagined it might be true. Turk was easily capable of killing him. "You want to help?"

"Yes!"

"Okay, where are we?"

"Oh. We're just north of San Francisco near Santa Rosa. This is a ranch about five miles outside of town. Take Holloway Road to get back to the freeway."

"And the keys to your car?"

"They're on the pegboard by the door to the garage. You can take the Porsche—it's fast."

Carl nodded. "Thanks." He stepped back.

"But—what about Sven! He needs help!" She gripped the bars of the cell, her eyes desperate.

"Tell you what," he said to her, "I'll call the police just before I go inside Turk's place. That way, if he kills me, you'll still be rescued. It's the best I can do." He turned to go.

"Wait! There's something you should know! About Turk!"

Carl turned back. He expected lies.

"Turk is dangerous. He'll kill you this time. He's afraid of nothing." She paused, biting her lip. "I shouldn't tell you this, but you should know that he's been kidnapping women and shipping them off to foreign countries as slaves. That's what he's going to do to DeeDee. No one's been able to figure out what's been happening to these girls, the police think it's a serial killer because no one ever hears from them again and no one finds the bodies. You can't prove it. Turk covers his tracks—the girls just disappear. But they're all alive! God, he'd kill me if he knew I told you."

Carl was stunned, then instantly furious. "You've known about this and you haven't told anyone? I should leave you locked up to die, just like you left those women to suffer at the hands of that madman!"

He stalked off, ignoring Gloria's entreaties. He mounted the stairs two at a time. In his haste, he nearly ran out to the garage naked, then stopped, shaking his head at his own foolishness. He rummaged through closets, looking for his clothes, but couldn't find them.

They were probably still in San Francisco. He did come across a pair of pants and a shirt of Sven's that fit him reasonably well, although the shoes were a size too big. He sucked his teeth in pain when he put on the shirt. He could feel the edges of the wounds from his whipping catching on the material. He was sure the blood was soaking through, leaving tiny trails across his back.

He grabbed the keys and jumped into the Porsche, grimacing when his back touched the seat. He figured it would take less than an hour to reach Turk's place. On the way, he mulled over what he would do when he got there. This time, he knew he had the advantage of surprise, but he wasn't about to go in armed with just a screwdriver, not after seeing Turk close up. Yet there wasn't time to buy a gun, even a shotgun. The paperwork would take too long. He had to get to DeeDee before she was shipped out. Of course, he had to call the police, but he really wanted to get there first.

He gunned the car, heading toward the freeway, thinking. By the time he hit the onramp, he thought he'd figured out a crude plan.

Chapter Nineteen

It was just past dusk when Carl reached Turk's neighborhood. He'd put his plan into action by stopping at a hardware store and a pay phone on the way. He parked a block away, took out the small plastic bag of items he'd purchased and strode quickly toward the house, looking over his shoulder for any unusual activity. He hoped he had timed this right. When he reached Turk's mansion, he snuck up the drive and climbed over the gate into the backyard. He hoped no one had spotted him.

He crept around the house, looking through the windows to check for Turk or Crystal. He had the advantage of being able to see in without being seen, provided he stayed away from the glow of the deck lights. He duck-walked around the house until he found the study that he'd been in a few days earlier. It was empty.

He tried raising the window. As expected, it was locked. Putting down the bag, he took out the roll of duct tape, tore off a couple of feet and stuck about six inches of it to the windowpane, right above the lock. He took out a glass cutter, and cut a crude circle around the tape. He tapped the glass with the round end of the cutter, wincing at the noise it made, although it probably didn't carry far in the vast house. He heard the glass crack then pulled at the tape, causing the section of come out in his hands.

As he was reaching in to unlock the window, he heard the squawk of a police radio nearby. Carl paused, scanning the sky and noticed dim red and blue flashes against the trees. He smiled to himself. He unlocked the window and raised it up. He crawled inside then took a few minutes to case the place. He hoped he might find a safe or some papers in the desk drawer that would incriminate Turk, but he doubted the man would be that dumb. Still, it was worth a try.

He heard the doorbell and nodded. The timing had been nearly perfect. He had called the police just minutes before he'd arrived at the mansion.

He was just about to give up his search and start for the door, when he happened to peek behind one of the paintings and noticed it was hinged on the side, rather than hung from above. He pulled it away from the wall and saw the safe set in the wall behind it. He put the painting back, then went to the door, opening it a crack and putting his ear to it.

Carl stood there, listening as Crystal then Turk talked to the police officers who had responded to the call about a kidnapped woman at this residence.

"Officer, I don't know what's going on here," Turk was saying in his smooth, urbane voice. "This must be some kind of prank. There's no one being kidnapped here."

Carl couldn't hear the murmur of the officer's reply and took a chance to peek through the crack in the door.

"Sure, you can come in and look around. I've got nothing to hide."

The two officers and Turk began a tour of the old house, starting with the opposite wing. When they disappeared from view, Carl sneaked out into the hall and approached the bookcase. When Crystal had opened it before, Carl couldn't tell which book she'd pulled, but thought it might've been on the third shelf from the top. It had seemed to be about chest-high to Crystal.

He went down the row, pulling down on the top corner of the volumes until he reached "Ivanhoe." Instantly, he heard a click and the door popped open. Carl made sure the door stayed wide open as he descended the stairs. In the gloom, he searched for a light switch but couldn't find one. But there was a small nightlight burning along one wall and that would have to do.

"DeeDee?" he called softly, squinting into the semidarkness. As he moved further into the room, he found this dungeon was similar to the one he'd been in earlier that day. Perhaps Gloria had modeled her chamber after her mentor's. There were implements of torture along one wall, the thick wooden post in the middle. The only differences were this basement was carpeted throughout, and against the far wall, a large X-brace stood, no doubt used to "train" reluctant slaves.

He spotted three cages along the far wall and went to them. Two were occupied. The women were naked, bound and gagged. "DeeDee?"

One of the women struggled in her bonds. Yes, thank God! It was her!

As he moved closer, he could tell that both women had plugs in their pussies and asses. Wires led from them to small machines outside the cells, where lights winked. It appeared to be some kind of programmed device for stimulating the women, he decided. Part of their training.

He quickly shut off both machines then looked around for keys to the cell. All the while, he kept his ears cocked for the sounds of the policemen upstairs.

The keys were on a hook on a nearby wall. He grabbed them and unlocked DeeDee's cell. He stripped off her gag and hugged her.

"Oh, thank god, Master! I thought you were dead!"

He untied her arms and she moved quickly to remove the horrid devices from her orifices. Carl tried not to look.

"I'm not your master, DeeDee, but we'll talk about that later. Do me a favor… Can you scream for me?"

DeeDee looked up, confused and terrified. "But he'll hear us! He'll kill you!"

"No, he won't. There's a couple of cops upstairs, looking for a kidnap victim right now. I called it in. If you scream, they'll come running down here and Turk will be busted. That is, unless you want to stay…"

DeeDee opened her mouth and gave the most bloodcurdling scream Carl had ever heard. He had to clap his hand over his ears. In seconds, he heard Turk's protesting voice, then thumps as the officers' boots hit the stairs.

"This way, officers," Carl called out, as he struggled to untie the soft ropes on DeeDee's feet.

But the officers made one crucial mistake. In their haste to come down and see what the screaming was about, they both ran ahead of Turk. The slave trader pushed the back of the second policeman hard, causing him to stumble into the man in front. Carl looked up to see both officers tumbling down the stairs. Turk slammed the door above them.

Carl ran to them. One of the officers had hurt his knee, but said he could still walk. Carl helped them up then explained who he was and what he was doing there. He had to talk fast, for the officers appeared ready to shoot somebody.

The injured officer introduced himself as Baldwin; the other man was Hobbs. Baldwin tried his radio, but the thick walls of the dungeon prevented any signal from getting out. While Baldwin limped over to help Carl free the second woman, Hobbs ran back upstairs to see if he could unlock the door.

Once freed, the second woman told the officers she was Betty Flanders, a student at Arizona State University who had vanished two weeks ago. The petite brunette with a Winona Ryder haircut said she had been walking across the quad at night, when someone snuck up behind her and clasped a smelly handkerchief across her face. She had passed out and awakened here.

"God! It was awful! The things they made me do!"

She was acutely embarrassed to be nude in front of the officer, so he kindly doffed his leather jacket and draped it over her shoulders. She hugged it tightly. DeeDee just stood there naked, seemingly unconcerned.

While Betty was telling her tale, Hobbs reported that the door required a key. Baldwin shouted up for him to use his radio while standing by the door, hoping the signal could penetrate the steel and wood and carry to the car, where it would be transmitted to the station.

"Yeah!" he shouted down a few seconds later. "I got 'em!"

"Great," Baldwin said. "Of course, we'll never live this down." He shook his head ruefully.

It took ten minutes for other officers to arrive. Carl had to shout through the bookcase, telling them to find "Ivanhoe." In seconds, they were free. The girls came up the stairs first, accompanied by the officers who hovered protectively around them. Hobbs had given his jacket to DeeDee, though she hadn't asked for it. In fact, Carl thought DeeDee was surprisingly subdued for just having been rescued from a life of servitude. Had Turk brainwashed her already?

Turk, of course, was gone. So was Crystal. No doubt he had some kind of escape plan mapped out. When Carl told them about the safe and led them to the room, he wasn't surprised to find it standing open, empty. He searched the desk for his wallet, but that was missing as well.

"Dammit! He got cash and whatever evidence was in there. Now we may never see him again," he said, bitterly disappointed. "He's probably heading for the airport."

"We'll put out an APB. If he's stupid enough to try and fly out of here, we'll get him," Baldwin told him.

Turk didn't seem stupid, but Carl didn't say anything.

At the station, Carl gave his story four or five times to a pair of suspicious detectives while victim's assistance people found clothes for DeeDee and Betty. Betty got on the phone to her parents, who were overjoyed at hearing their daughter was safe. The police asked DeeDee if she had anyone to call, a mother or father, but she just shook her head.

"I've got no one," she said simply. Carl knew that wasn't true—her mother was still alive, though estranged, but he decided not to press it.

"Hey," he said, pulling her close. "You've got me." She hugged him fiercely. It was the first real emotion he'd seen from her since their rescue. Carl's back burned where she touched him, but he made no mention of it, so thrilled to have found her before she'd been sold and flown to god knows where.

The Santa Rosa Sheriff's Department called and reported they had found Gloria and Sven at their ranch. They were both in custody. Gloria was demanding that Carl be arrested for assaulting Sven.

"Bitch," he muttered.

One of the detectives, named Reilly, suggested Carl let them photograph the marks on his back to help prove the case. They took him into a separate room. An assistant D.A. came in with a Polaroid, reminding Carl of the Polaroid pictures that Gloria had of him in a compromising position. No doubt they would become part of the trial record. He shuddered. As he eased his shirt off, the A.D.A. and Reilly both gasped.

"Jesus H. Christ," Reilly breathed while the A.D.A snapped a couple of pictures. "How did you survive that?"

Carl just shook his head, not knowing how to answer that. Paramedics were called in to treat his wounds. He refused to go to the hospital.

It took several hours for processing. Gloria and Sven were held on charges of kidnapping and torture. A warrant was put out for Turk's arrest, and Crystal was wanted for questioning. They had failed to turn up at any of the local airports, as Carl had feared. He assumed Turk had chartered a plane or was driving to a hideout, biding his time until he could safely escape.

Either way, Carl doubted Turk would remain in the country for long. It bothered him that they had been so close to capturing him, but he had slipped through their fingers. However, his disappointment paled to the righteous anger displayed by the officers' sergeant, who yelled at them in the middle of the bullpen over such a boneheaded move.

"What if he'd pulled a gun on you while your backs were turned, huh?!" he'd bellowed. "You'd both be dead and I'd have to explain to your widows what idiots you'd been! Do you think that'd be an easy job? Huh?"

The contrite officers just stood there with heads bowed. Carl suspected they would be walking traffic beats before the week was out.

That reminded him. "Officer — what day is it?" In all the confusion of the last few days, he'd completely forgotten his promise to his client.

"Why, Friday — almost Saturday," he said, looking at the clock, which read 11:34.

Shit! "I've got to use the phone." Carl hated to call his client so late, but he might be up still, fuming over the project that didn't get done.

Reilly handed him his cell phone without a word and asked if he needed some privacy. Carl became aware that he was still shirtless, so he began putting it back on even as he shook his head.

As expected, his client was furious — until he heard Carl's incredible story. He almost didn't believe him until Carl told him to read the paper in the morning. He signed off, promising to have the completed materials to the printer first thing Monday. The client, much more subdued, said that would be fine. It turned out his hard and fast deadline could be moved a couple of days after all.

It was after midnight when Carl and DeeDee were allowed to leave. It was too late to go home, so they stayed at a hotel. Carl used Gloria's money to buy a change of clothes for both of them at the hotel boutique. He offered to buy underwear for DeeDee, but she just shook her head and smiled for the first time since her rescue.

"DeeDee, I'm so glad to have you back safe and sound! I was really worried about you."

She nodded, her face blank. "Thank you," she said softly.

"What's wrong? What happened to you in there?" Carl hated to ask, but he wanted to know.

"It was...overwhelming. I didn't know what to think. And then, I stopped thinking at all. It was easier that way."

Carl caught himself before he could press for more details. There would be time for that later, he decided. For now, he was just glad she was back.

"Are you hungry?"

The question seemed to surprise her. "Um, I don't know. I guess."

Perhaps Turk had decided everything for her, including when to eat. And for that matter what to eat. "Would you like me to get you something? We could order room service. Anything you want." He showed her the menu.

She glanced at it then shook her head. "I'm not that hungry. Maybe I'll just have some peanuts from the mini-bar."

"Sure. Let me get some for you." He jumped up, trying to show her that she didn't have to obey anyone anymore. He was happy to fetch something for her. When he turned his back, he heard DeeDee gasp. He turned back, concerned, thinking she was having a flashback to her ordeal. Instead, she pointed to him.

"Your back."

"Oh. That." He turned and looked over his shoulder. A red line had seeped through his brand-new shirt. He cursed and eased it off, planning to soak it in the sink.

She gasped again when she saw the bandages over his back. "I'm sorry. So sorry."

"Why? This isn't your fault."

"But it is. Master Turk or Gloria wouldn't've hurt you if it wasn't for me."

"That's nonsense. I'm just glad I was there to help. Think what your life would be like if Turk had come for you before I met you."

She was silent, apparently thinking about that horror. Carl splashed water on the shirt, rubbing away the bloodstain. He felt guilty too. If he hadn't explored her darker side, perhaps she would've been strong enough to resist Turk's orders. Then again, knowing how big Turk was, he might've just kidnapped her, like he did to so many others.

It worried Carl that the police hadn't yet tracked Turk down. By now, he'd probably holed up somewhere, under the protection of another slaver, or was on his way out of the country. Carl had told the police about Hank—with any luck, the bald club owner might know where Turk would hide. He hoped they would make the treacherous man sweat.

He returned to the room and went to DeeDee's side. Carl told her he felt much better and he did, but he suspected it was more because she seemed to be coming out of her shell, becoming a bit more like the DeeDee he knew and loved.

DeeDee was exhausted by her ordeal. She said she wanted to take a shower and go to bed. When she came out of the shower, he went in and cleaned up in the sink, careful not to get his back wet. By the time he came out again, she was in bed, asleep.

Carl slipped in beside her and rested his hand gently on her hip. She had put on an oversized t-shirt he had bought for her and the material felt soft and warm to the touch. She snuggled a little closer and Carl smiled just before he fell asleep.

Chapter Twenty

Carl's car had been towed to the impound lot after a passing officer had spotted it in front of the hydrant near Turk's house. Despite the kidnapping, the police didn't offer to cover the cost of the ticket or the storage fees, so Carl paid it using the last of Gloria's money and drove the car back to the hotel. DeeDee was waiting in the lobby, dressed in jeans and a blouse. She seemed anxious to get out of there.

Carl had called the police before he left, telling them where they'd be. Reilly thanked him and said they'd call when Turk was in custody. "It's only a matter of time," he assured Carl. "The guy can't disappear."

The drove south, stopping for lunch at a restaurant near Gilroy then took another break in San Luis Obispo, just to walk around and stretch their legs. Carl was in no hurry. He hoped the drive would bring DeeDee around, as she still seemed somewhat distant. *Give her time*, he told himself.

They pulled into Santa Barbara just before six, and headed for Carl's house. He had offered to take her to her apartment instead, but she'd said no immediately. The idea of being alone in that place clearly frightened her.

"I'd feel safer at your place. Is that all right?"

All right! As if she even had to ask. "It's perfect," he said.

The house looked inviting to Carl, like an old friend. He parked in the driveway and helped her out. "I know you don't have much in the way of clothes, but tomorrow, if you're up to it, we can swing by your place and get some things."

She nodded, her eyes thoughtful. She focused on Carl's face. "Thank you," she whispered, making Carl feel like a hero all over again.

"I wasn't going to abandon you there. No way. I'm just glad I got there in time."

She touched his cheek then followed him inside. They had no luggage. "I don't know about you, but I'm hungry again," he told her. "Would you like me to fix you a sandwich?" He stretched his cramped muscles. When he glanced over at DeeDee, she was standing stock-still, her face drained of color.

"Well, well, what a nice surprise," a growling voice said.

Carl whirled around, eyes wide, to see Turk standing in the doorway to the kitchen, a gun in one hand. His mouth dropped open. Beside him, he heard DeeDee drop to her knees on the carpet with a thud.

Turk was no longer that calm, cool character Carl had met that day in the library. Now his face was drawn, his scalp sweating and his anger palpable. Carl felt his knees go weak.

As Turk came into the living room, Crystal appeared. She wore shorts and a t-shirt that said, "Monterey Bay Aquarium." Perhaps they had hid there in plain sight, just a couple of tourists.

"The police are looking everywhere for you, Turk," Carl said, trying to keep his voice calm. "They're coming by here as well—the cops called ahead to the Santa

Barbara Police." It was a lie, but he hoped it might cause Turk to flee.

No such luck.

"Don't worry, we'll be long gone by the time they find your body." He grinned, then immediately glowered again. "You really fucked up my plans, you know that?"

"So what are you trying to prove here? You know this is a huge risk for you. If you kill us, you won't get a hundred miles from here before they catch you. They'll have your description out to every cop around."

"True—I might get caught. But at least I'll have had the satisfaction of killing you first."

Carl felt dizzy and sick. That Turk was going to kill him, he was certain. There was nothing he could say to scare him off.

"What about DeeDee? Can't you just let her go? Haven't you tortured her enough?"

"Let her go?" He laughed, a deep booming sound. "Oh, no, DeeDee belongs to me. I have big plans for her."

Carl glanced over to see DeeDee kneeling there, legs apart, back erect, hands crossed behind her, as she'd been taught. She seemed to have fallen right back into her controlled state. He wondered if she even knew he was here. If Turk shot him, would she react? Would she be sad?

Turk came forward. The gun in his fist loomed large. Carl could see eternity in the black hole of the barrel.

"If you shoot that gun in here, the neighbors are bound to hear," he said, desperation creeping into his voice. He grasped at straws. "Besides, it's not really the way you'd like to kill me, is it?" Carl held his breath.

Turk shrugged. "One way's as good as another." But he hesitated.

Carl jumped at the slim chance he felt he had. After all, he had nothing to lose. "I'll bet you'd really rather take me on man-to-man, right? Get some of that anger out of your system? Think about how much more satisfactory it'd be to feel your fists breaking my bones, instead of just pulling a trigger. Hell, a woman could pull a trigger."

Carl knew he'd appealed to Turk's machismo. The big man's eyes widened then narrowed. One corner of his mouth went up in a mocking sneer. "You think you could take me?"

Carl shrugged elaborately. "I'd at least have a fighting chance, wouldn't I?"

Turk studied him for a long few seconds. "Crystal," he barked.

The Asian came around quickly, bowing her head. "Yes, Master?"

"Get the girl." She ran over to DeeDee and helped her to her feet. Bringing her arms around behind her, Crystal held them tight in her grasp then walked her over to Turk's side.

"Stand in the kitchen. Find something to tie her up with. Make sure she watches this. I'm going to beat her boyfriend to death. DeeDee will know then who's in charge."

Turk handed her the pistol, then casually mentioned. "Oh, and if by some miracle he happens to win, shoot him."

Carl's heart lurched. His slim chance had just withered to nothing. If by some stroke of luck he managed to defeat this mountain of a man, he had no doubt that the loyal slave would try to shoot him. Would DeeDee try to stop her, or would she just stand there in a fog?

He had no time to think about it. Turk swung a heavy right hand at his head, expecting to end the fight suddenly. Carl ducked, pivoted and drove his own right hand as hard as he could into Turk's stomach. It was like hitting a wall of muscle. Turk grunted and said, "You'll have to do better than that, little man."

Jesus! Carl thought. *This guy is built like a truck!*

He felt his adrenaline kick in. Turk reached out with his meaty left hand and tried to grab Carl. He parried it then drove his left foot hard against Turk's knee. The knee gave slightly and Carl heard Turk curse. Then Turk twisted toward him, closing his right hand over Carl's upper arm. Carl found himself being drawn up into a bear hug. He knew Turk could crush his ribcage if he managed to lock his hands behind him.

He slapped both hands over Turk's ears, knowing it would cause excruciating pain to his eardrums and the big man dropped Carl. As soon as his feet touched the ground, he drove his right knee into Turk's groin.

Turk bellowed and jerked backwards, folding at the waist. Carl tried to follow up, but Turk backhanded him, sending him flying into the couch. As he scrambled to his feet, Turk tossed an end table at him, causing him to fall again. He struggled to stand, but tripped over a table leg. He caught himself with one hand on the couch then looked up to see Turk pick up an ottoman and hurl it toward him. Carl fell back again awkwardly, feeling a sharp pain in his left arm when he tried to catch himself.

He rolled away, kicked his leg clear and stood up, just as Turk came at him with another roundhouse right. Carl got his left arm up just in time to block and felt it give way with an audible crack, sending shooting pains up to his shoulder. The punch, barely deflected, sent him reeling. The room spun and he found himself on his back, looking up at the murderous face of Turk. He held the wooden coffee table overhead, ready to smash it down on Carl's head.

In a last, desperate act, Carl kicked at Turk's leg, trying to knock him off-balance. It was a delaying tactic, he knew. With his left arm broken, he couldn't stop the big man. Turk shrugged the blow off and aimed anew.

There was a sudden sharp report and Turk stopped in mid-action. His expression changed. He looked confused. He turned. Carl followed his gaze to see DeeDee, holding the pistol out in front of her, her face stained with tears. He looked down and saw Crystal, propped up against the cabinets, holding her head.

"Whaa…?" He couldn't believe she'd gotten the gun away from Crystal.

There came another gunshot and Turk staggered, then let the coffee table slip from his grasp. Carl yanked his legs out of the way just in time before it crashed to the floor. Turk took a step toward the kitchen, his face blank.

"Dee…?"

"Shut up, asshole," she said. She fired once more and Turk pitched over backwards. He groaned once then lay still.

Carl stared at the girl he thought he knew, not sure what to expect. He waited and watched as she slowly let the gun drop, then relaxed her grip. The gun clunked to the floor. DeeDee began to cry. Great, wracking sobs. She could no longer stand up, so she sank to the floor, weeping, covering her face with her hands.

Carl stood on shaky legs then went to DeeDee. He kept a wary eye on Crystal, but she seemed to be in shock in the corner. He could see blood trickling from her nose.

"DeeDee, are you okay? Are you with me?"

Her eyes came back into focus and she stared at him.

"Yeah."

"How did you get the gun away from her?"

"Elbow." Then she noticed his crooked left arm. "You're hurt."

Carl nodded. "Yeah."

Her gaze went from it to Turk, lying on the floor, then back to Carl.

"Jesus. Is he really dead?"

"I think so." He glanced over at Crystal. She wasn't going to be much help. "Listen, I'm going to call the police. Will you keep an eye on Crystal?"

Her eyes locked onto his. "Okay."

He picked up the gun with his right hand and placed it on the counter by the phone. He lifted the receiver.

"Is it really over?"

He turned to see DeeDee staring at him, as if she couldn't believe what she had just done. "Yes. It's over."

Chapter Twenty-one

For the second time in two days, Carl and DeeDee found themselves surrounded by police, answering questions. At first, they didn't know what to make of the scene: A large, muscular man dead on the floor, shot three times, and two young women and a man with an impossible story to relate.

Once the Santa Barbara detectives talked to their counterparts in San Francisco, they came around. They were excited to be part of a high-profile bust. And all they had to do was show up.

While paramedics splinted Carl's arm in preparation for taking him to the hospital, a detective came over with a cell phone. "Detective Reilly wants to talk to you."

Carl took the phone in his good hand. "Yeah?"

"Sorry about the mess you got into down there," Reilly said. "We should've thought to have someone check out your house. Dammit, we knew he had your wallet."

"It never occurred to me, either. I figured he'd be long gone."

"We should've guessed he might be so angry at you to make you pay for the loss of his business."

"Yeah, that's the way it looks."

"Well, I know you gotta go to the hospital. But I wanted to tell you — you got a lot of guts."

"I was lucky. If DeeDee hadn't shot him, I'd be dead now."

"Yeah. You've got yourself a great gal there. This Crystal woman bothers me. I doubt that's her real name. We're trying to track down her family now. Did she ever say anything to you about where she came from?"

"No. I just assumed she was part of Turk's world from the beginning. How else could she stay with him so long?" Even as he said it, Carl thought of DeeDee's blank expression and obedient behavior. Given enough time, she could've ended up just like Crystal—or whatever her name really was.

"Well, I've got the police down there helping us, so we'll figure it out. Is DeeDee all right?"

"She seems to be, although she's in shock, I think. They're taking her to the hospital too, just for a checkup."

"Good. Well, you guys take care. I'm glad you're okay."

At the hospital, an orthopedic surgeon was called in to set Carl's arm. When he was finally released, a bulky cast bouncing in a sling, he went straight to DeeDee's room.

She was lying back, the bed tilted up. When she saw his face, she smiled and held out a hand.

"Wow, you look much better," he said immediately, taking her hand in his.

"I feel better. They gave me something. Valium, I think. I'll be released in a bit. Ohh, look at your arm. Does it hurt?"

"Only when I bowl," he said, trying to make her laugh.

"Sit here." He obliged and sat on the edge of her bed. She put her hand on his thigh. "You are an amazing man, Carl Harman. I hope you know that."

"Aw, shucks," he joked, then turned serious. "I wasn't going to leave you there."

"And I thank you."

"I thank you, too. I'd be dead if it wasn't for you."

"You're welcome."

He sat beside her on the bed, holding her hand, thinking how lucky he was to have met her.

"DeeDee—" He stopped.

"Yeah?"

"This lifestyle. It really sucks you in, doesn't it? I mean, it's kind of dangerous, and yet, kind of exciting too."

She nodded. "Yes, it is. I hadn't realized how much a part of my life it had become until I spent time in Turk's dungeon. I don't think I ever want to experience that level of intensity again." She rubbed his arm. "It's better as a game."

He nodded. "Yeah. But it's a game I don't want to play for a while."

"Well, no. At least, not until your arm heals."

That surprised him. "Really? You aren't mad at me?"

Her puzzled look seemed genuine. "What would I be mad about?"

"Well, you know. The trip to the mall and all…" He felt his face grow red.

She shook her head. "You kidding me? I never had such orgasms in my life! It was like taking a drug or something. You know, if we could bottle that somehow, we'd make a fortune."

"Yeah, but … Didn't you feel exploited? Used?"

"Yes and no. Yes, of course I did — and that was the point, wasn't it? To be, um, subservient, is a big part of my life for a reason. I like it — with the right man. That's why I didn't feel used, because I was with you. I did feel used with Turk. He didn't take any of my feelings into account. With you, I felt like you were watching out for me all the time. I could just let myself go and enjoy it. I'm sure if you went too far, I'd lose that feeling, but you never did. You took me right to the edge."

"So you're telling me that you think it's okay for a woman to be treated that way?"

She shook her head. "Not any woman. Just me." She dipped her head. "I guess I should've told you that first night that I was kinda crazy."

"No, you aren't — "

"Hush, it's okay. I don't mean crazy like I should be locked up. I just mean odd. Strange. Twisted — but in a good way. Does that make sense?"

"Well, yes, but after getting tangled up with Turk, I figured you'd hate that whole scene. And because I was part of it, you might be angry with me too."

"How could I, after you saved me? Do you know what it was like for me there? Waiting for orders from Turk, being made to do whatever I was told, regardless of how I felt?" She wiped away a tear. "I'm telling you, Carl, I was on my way to becoming a zombie. That's the way men like Turk like women. Not you. You liked me for what I was inside as well as outside."

Carl could feel his own tears coming now and he didn't care. He'd never met someone like DeeDee and he wasn't sure if he deserved her.

"Listen, I'm going to take you home to my place and take care of you. I want you to feel secure again. Then we can talk about what we want to do about…lifestyle choices." He waved his hand vaguely in the air.

DeeDee smiled then shook her head. "No, Carl. You're not going to take care of me. I'm fine, really. You're the one with the broken arm. I intend to take care of you. Feed you, wash you, even do some of the heavy lifting if I have to."

His eyes were blurred by tears and he found himself grinning like a fool. "What about your place?"

She shuddered. "I don't want to go back there right now. The way Turk burst in that day—" She shook her head. "You don't mind if I stay with you?"

"I was hoping you'd say that." He looked around. "Now where's that doctor? I want to take you home."

Epilogue

Carl flexed his left arm, which appeared shrunken and white compared to the other one. He was glad to finally have the damn cast off after two months, but now he'd have to do some serious physical therapy to bring it back to normal.

"Whaddya think?" He held his arms out, side by side for inspection.

DeeDee, sitting next to him on the couch, leaned down, her mouth pursed in a comic exaggeration of distaste. "Eww. I hope you're not going to touch me with that thing."

"Hey!" He took his arms back in mock offense.

"Oh, stop. You know I love you, even if you had a wooden leg."

Carl took her hand, noting the sharp contrast in tone between their arms. "I just need a little tan. Besides, I figured you'd prefer tender flesh to that hard cast."

"Yeah, that was getting old. I'm tired of always being on top."

"Some women really like that. They say it gives them power over a man."

DeeDee grinned. "I think I'm ready to let you be the one with the power for a change."

He leaned over and kissed her. Her lips were soft and full of promise; her breath caught in her throat. "I'll see what I can do to vary our routine."

"Whatever you say…Master."

"Oh, are we back to that now?"

"Well, it's been two months. I'm hoping now that your arm is better, you might want to experiment a little."

Carl had expected this. While their lovemaking had been very satisfying, he'd felt there was something missing, something adventurous and naughty. "Hmm. I have an idea. To celebrate the removal of the cast, I'll take you out to dinner." He watched her face brighten. "Naturally," he continued, "you'll want to wear undergarments."

She silently shook her head.

He opened his eyes wide. "You're refusing?"

"It's just so damn hot, I hate to wear them. They pinch me and ride up."

"Only Naughty Girls refuse to wear underwear."

He watched her eyes grow large, luminous. "What—" She licked her lips. "What would happen if I refused to wear them?"

"Well, you'd have to be punished, of course. We can't have you refusing orders, now can we?"

"What k-kind of punishments…Master?"

"For starters, I'd have you remove all your clothes and assume the position. If you continued to refuse, I'd have to get out the ruler."

"And, if that didn't work?"

"Then I'd have to assume you liked parading around half-dressed like a Naughty Girl. Perhaps you'd learn your lesson if you went out to dinner in a short skirt, flashing the waiters."

DeeDee opened her mouth then closed it again. Carl could sense the heat building up in her. Her neck flushed pink.

"Well?"

"Whatever you say, Master. Just please don't make me wear underwear."

Carl pretended to look disappointed, yet he enjoyed the rush of sexual energy the little exchange had created. This woman was a pistol! Even after her ordeal, she still liked the games they played.

"Go get the ruler," he said. "And when you come back, you'd better be prepared to assume the position!"

She smiled, rose gracefully and left the room.

Carl felt his cock press against his pants. He looked down. "Aren't you the naughty one?" he smiled.

Enjoy this excerpt from:
WANTED: KEPT WOMAN

© Copyright J. W. McKenna, 2004

The women flew from store to store, trying on outfits and shoes and giggling like high school kids. Suzanne bought a new dress, plus a skirt and a pair of shoes. She used up her clothing allowance for the next six months.

"Don't worry about it," Wendy had told her. "When you meet your sugar daddy, this won't matter."

"Oh, yeah, right," she retorted. But she did feel more attractive now. The small changes had helped break her out of the doldrums.

"Here, the new issue's out," Wendy said suddenly, grabbing a free *Bayside Weekly* off the rack. "Let's find you a man, okay?"

Suzanne blushed and looked around. "Come on, Wen. Not so loud. You make me sound desperate!"

Wendy looked up from the paper. "Oh, sorry." She grinned. "But we can't let another day pass without sharing your new look with a brand new man!"

"I'm an independent woman, I don't need…" she started to mutter, but Wendy had already walked away. She followed. They sat down on a bench, their heads together as they read the ads.

"Here's one, '*SWPM ISO fun-loving, smart, athletic SWF ages 26-36. NS preferred*'."

"Nah, 'athletic' means he doesn't want anyone who's…" Suzanne didn't want to say the "F" word as she no longer thought of herself that way. Yes, five pounds made that much difference. "…not really skinny."

"Oh, I don't know about that. You look great. Okay, try this one, '*SWDM seeks SWF for fun, walks in the park, movies, games and possible LTR. Must like kids*'." She paused. "Uh oh."

Wendy put the down the paper and both women looked at each other. Simultaneously, they shrieked, "He wants a mom!"

"Yeah," Suzanne gasped. "He probably has four rotten kids and sole custody!"

"Can you imagine who'd respond to that ad? She'd be a woman with three rotten kids whose husband just ran off!"

They laughed and slapped their thighs. Other shoppers looked at them as if they were crazy women.

"Okay," Wendy said, tears in her eyes from laughter, "I'm willing to concede maybe that's not a good one!"

She began reading again. Suzanne was ready to chuck the paper in the trash and head back to work. It was amusing to read them, sure, but to actually answer—

"Hey!"

Wendy looked up from the paper. "Here's that ad again. The one you were talking about last week." She showed Suzanne the paper.

Wanted: Kept woman…

"Wow! Two weeks in a row! He must be really desperate!"

"Or maybe he just signed up for two weeks originally, not knowing how many responses he'd get. You never know," Wendy pointed out.

"Yeah, well, he probably looks like a toad. Or he's a perv."

"Well, I'm going to call to find out." Wendy fished her cell phone out of her purse.

Suzanne gasped. "No! You can't!" She started to rise. Wendy caught her arm and pulled her back down, then punched in some numbers. Suzanne tried to get away, but Wendy grabbed her arm again and held it.

"Hello? I'm calling about the ad? Uh-uh." She listened as Suzanne sat there, eyes wide.

"Yes, I can do that. Okay, here's the email address…"

Suzanne was stunned to hear Wendy give out Suzanne's email address. "You—!"

"Shh!" she said quickly, her hand over the mouthpiece. To the phone she said, "No, someone was talking. It's all right."

Wendy made a few more agreeable comments and hung up. She smiled at Suzanne.

"Well? What? What'd they say?"

"Oh, now you're curious? You, the girl who'd never answer another personal ad?"

Suzanne brought her hands up and made choking gestures in mid-air.

"Okay, okay," Wendy laughed. "She was very nice…"

"She?"

"She was the secretary. Or personal assistant. I'm not sure. Rebecca something. I'm telling you, Suze, this guy does sound rich."

"Why don't you date him then?"

Wendy put her hand over her heart. "Because I'm doing this for you. I know you'd never do this for yourself. You need a push and I'm pushing. Look at you. In a week you've lost some weight, gotten a whole new look and I'll bet you're feeling much better about yourself, right?"

Suzanne had to agree.

"So think of this as the next step in making the New Suzanne."

"I don't want to date this stranger! You're the one complaining about men lately! Why not go after him yourself?"

"Well, I could. We both could."

"What do you mean? A threesome?"

Wendy laughed. "God, no. I love ya, dear, but not like that! No, the secretary said we have to fill out a short questionnaire and send in a photo in order to get to the next step."

"Oh, right. I'll be sure and do that!" She'd already dismissed the idea as dangerous and stupid.

"Oh, no you don't," Wendy said. "I'm going to make sure you fill it out. And if you won't send in a photo, I'm sure I can find one in my collection somewhere..." She paused and looked toward the ceiling. "I can think of a time when you got drunk in Santa Barbara..."

"You wouldn't!"

"I would. Look, girlfriend, I'm going to bust you out of your rut if it's the last thing I do, okay? You don't have to marry the guy or even date him more than once, but you gotta get out there and try, you know?"

Suzanne nodded, secretly pleased that Wendy was pushing her into this. She would be far too shy to promote herself. Despite her grave misgivings, she thought she'd humor her friend and let her do this for her. It wouldn't go any further than this first step.

"Okay, but only if you fill it out on yourself as well."

Wendy shrugged. "What the hell. It could be fun. If it will make you do it, I'll do it too."

About the author:

J.W. McKenna is a former journalist who took up penning erotic romance stories after years of trying to ignore an overly dramatic—and often overheated—imagination. McKenna is married and lives in the Midwest, where polite people would be shocked if they knew what kind of writing was being done in their town.

J. W. welcomes mail from readers. You can write to her c/o Ellora's Cave Publishing at 1337 Commerce Drive, Suite 13, Stow OH 44224.

Also by J. W. McKenna:

Darkest Hour
Trackers - *The Hunted anthology*
Slave Planet
Lord of Avalon
The Cameo
Wanted: Kept Woman

Why an electronic book?

We live in the Information Age — an exciting time in the history of human civilization in which technology rules supreme and continues to progress in leaps and bounds every minute of every hour of every day. For a multitude of reasons, more and more avid literary fans are opting to purchase e-books instead of paperbacks. The question to those not yet initiated to the world of electronic reading is simply: *why?*

1. *Price.* An electronic title at Ellora's Cave Publishing runs anywhere from 40-75% less than the cover price of the <u>exact same title</u> in paperback format. Why? Cold mathematics. It is less expensive to publish an e-book than it is to publish a paperback, so the savings are passed along to the consumer.

2. *Space.* Running out of room to house your paperback books? That is one worry you will never have with electronic novels. For a low one-time cost, you can purchase a handheld computer designed specifically for e-reading purposes. Many e-readers are larger than the average handheld, giving you plenty of screen room. Better yet, hundreds of titles can be stored within your new library — a single microchip. (Please note that Ellora's Cave does not endorse any specific brands. You can check our website at www.ellorascave.com for customer recommendations we make available to new consumers.)

3. *Mobility.* Because your new library now consists of only a microchip, your entire cache of books can be taken with you wherever you go.

4. *Personal preferences are accounted for.* Are the words you are currently reading too small? Too large? Too...**ANNOYING**? Paperback books cannot be modified according to personal preferences, but e-books can.

5. *Innovation.* The way you read a book is not the only advancement the Information Age has gifted the literary community with. There is also the factor of what you can read. Ellora's Cave Publishing will be introducing a new line of interactive titles that are available in e-book format only.

6. *Instant gratification.* Is it the middle of the night and all the bookstores are closed? Are you tired of waiting days—sometimes weeks—for online and offline bookstores to ship the novels you bought? Ellora's Cave Publishing sells instantaneous downloads 24 hours a day, 7 days a week, 365 days a year. Our e-book delivery system is 100% automated, meaning your order is filled as soon as you pay for it.

Those are a few of the top reasons why electronic novels are displacing paperbacks for many an avid reader. As always, Ellora's Cave Publishing welcomes your questions and comments. We invite you to email us at service@ellorascave.com or write to us directly at: 1337 Commerce Drive, Suite 13, Stow OH 44224.

Discover for yourself why readers can't get enough of the multiple award-winning publisher Ellora's Cave. Whether you prefer e-books or paperbacks, be sure to visit EC on the web at www.ellorascave.com for an erotic reading experience that will leave you breathless.

WWW.ELLORASCAVE.COM